**Joelle shuddered as Leo lifted his head, looked down on her, looked to see her spread out before him.**

She felt strangely like a sacrificial offering and it crossed her mind—fleetingly—that this was how it would have been on her wedding night if she'd waited, except she wouldn't have been half so attracted, half so turned on. Much better her first time is now, with Leo. Much better she do this her way, have something like this be her choice, within her control.

"I'm losing you," he said, his voice so husky it rasped across her senses, stirring her all over again.

"No. I'm here," she said, gathering her courage. "I want you."

# THE PRINCESS BRIDES

*For duty, for money…for passion!*

Enjoy the new trilogy from rising star author
Jane Porter!

Meet the Royals—the Ducasse family:
Chantal, Niccolette and Joelle. Step inside their
world and watch as three beautiful, independent
and very different princesses find their
own way to love and happiness.

This is the last book in Jane's marvelous
Princess Brides trilogy:

*The Sultan's Bought Bride* (#2418)

*The Greek's Royal Mistress* (#2424)

*The Italian's Virgin Princess* (#2430)

Available only from Harlequin Presents®

# Jane Porter

## THE ITALIAN'S VIRGIN PRINCESS

THEPRINCESSBRIDES

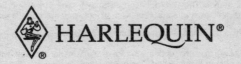

# HARLEQUIN®

TORONTO • NEW YORK • LONDON
AMSTERDAM • PARIS • SYDNEY • HAMBURG
STOCKHOLM • ATHENS • TOKYO • MILAN • MADRID
PRAGUE • WARSAW • BUDAPEST • AUCKLAND

For Elizabeth Boyle, great author and friend.
Thanks for your faith in me.

ISBN 0-373-12430-9

THE ITALIAN'S VIRGIN PRINCESS

First North American Publication 2004.

Copyright © 2004 by Jane Porter.

www.eHarlequin.com

**Printed in U.S.A.**

# PROLOGUE

*The Ducasse Palace, Porto, Melio*

PRINCESS JOELLE DUCASSE studied the sealed letter she'd left on her grandfather's desk. Identical copies of the letter were being couriered to her sisters, Nicolette in Baraka, and Chantal in Greece.

The heavy cream envelope with the gold Palace seal suddenly looked ominous on Grandpapa's desk.

*He'd be so hurt,* she thought, feeling tears well up. *He wouldn't understand.*

But then, she didn't even understand why she felt so desperate to get away, to escape Melio and the glare of publicity and the camera lenses. She'd never found it comfortable living in the public eye but since Grandmama's death it'd gotten worse. So much worse.

The media wouldn't—couldn't—let her grieve privately. They were there documenting every outing, every appearance, capturing Joelle's weekly visit to her grandmother's grave on film, capturing the sheen of tears in her eyes as she left the royal cemetery, capturing her shell-shocked expression as she climbed into the waiting car.

There was no privacy, no respect, and no time to hide her hurt. Or her confusion.

Grandmama's death had triggered all sorts of pain, pain that must have been buried deep inside of her since her parents' death eighteen years ago. And those tabloid photos, those sensationalized articles, Queen Astrid's Death Rocks The Youngest Princess, only made the confusion worse.

Truthfully, she didn't know what to feel. She didn't even feel. Sometime in the last six months, in the months between Grandmama's funeral and now, she'd lost all feeling, all hope, all courage.

How could she live a public life...a life of public service...if she didn't even know who she was? If she didn't even know *what* she was?

Joelle reached for the envelope on Grandpapa's desk, and her fingers brushed his antique leather blotter, a blotter that had been in the family for over a hundred years, the leather soft and worn, the felt pad replaced numerous times and tears filled her eyes.

She felt so conflicted. So much in knots.

Joelle loved the old leather blotter, loved Grandpapa's handsome paneled study, loved everything about the old limestone palace and she knew intellectually why she needed to marry and remain here—Nic had married the sultan and couldn't return to Melio, and Chantal had married a commoner and the Greek couldn't become king—but she couldn't imagine assuming more duty, more responsibility without recovering her composure first.

She needed a break. Space. Desperately needed privacy. The palace felt so empty without Grandmama, and while she adored Grandpapa, it was Grandmama who'd always counseled her, Grandmama she'd talked to. And now without Grandmama here, she couldn't bear it. Couldn't bear the emptiness, the loneliness, the uncertainty of her future, and yet Joelle knew it was time she started to come to grips with the loss. Even if it meant dealing with the grief her way, without everybody watching, without everybody talking.

Joelle left the letter where it was.

*I'm sorry, Grandpapa. Forgive me.*

You're only going for a year, she told herself, turning away from the desk and heading for the door. It's not forever. You'll be back in twelve months, you'll marry Prince Luigi Borgarde and life will continue as it should.

But six hours later as she settled into a coach seat on a small European carrier, sunglasses on, a hat pulled down low on her head, she was still trying to shake the guilt and focus on the positives.

She'd have twelve months to find peace, twelve months to come to grips with Grandmama's death, twelve months to grieve without being the focus of cameras and paparazzi.

And yet as the hours passed and Joelle struggled to get comfortable in her narrow coach seat, she wished for just one moment that she'd traveled the old way, traveled as a princess usually did—whisked in and out of security, private customs, private lounges, hidden behind the broad shoulders of bodyguards and airport security. Private protectors. Public defenders. Plainclothes police and government sharpshooters ever vigilant on behalf the royal family's safety. Security.

But that was the problem, Joelle thought, tugging her thin fuzzy blanket higher around her shoulders. There was no way to be Princess Joelle without the cameras, without the security, without the palace protocol. And as long as she remained Princess Joelle Ducasse, everyone would have too much information, would assume they knew everything about her.

But people didn't really know her. They only knew what the media wrote. They only knew what the palace PR people told them.

They didn't know her real dreams. Or the depth of her emotion. They didn't know how much she longed for choice. For independence. For freedom.

Her older sister, Chantal, said personal choice was overrated, not an essential, and certainly not a guarantee when one's last name was Ducasse and your lineage dated back to the late thirteenth century.

But Joelle didn't want to be a Ducasse. She'd had enough of the Ducasse lifestyle. All she wanted was to be a regular person. Private. Independent. Self-sufficient.

For one year she was going to be a regular Jo.

# CHAPTER ONE

*New Orleans, Eleven months later*

"A DRINK, Miss d'Ville?"

The question, asked by a distinctly male voice, a very deep, very quiet voice, sent a ripple of unease through Joelle. Voices like that only came from years of power.

Positions of authority, the kind of authority she'd left behind in Europe. Joelle turned reluctantly, more than reluctantly, knowing by his voice that it was him.

*Him.*

The one who'd sat in the front row tonight, just left of stage center.

The one who'd distracted her all night with his intense gaze, a gaze that never seemed to leave her.

Twice she'd lost her place in the middle of a song. Twice she'd stood there on stage in the purple and blue gel lights utterly blank—losing all thought, all memory, all words. She'd never forgotten lyrics like that. She'd never stared out at a dark sea of audience and wondered what she was doing with a microphone before.

But it hadn't been an entirely dark sea. She'd seen one face, one man the entire time, and his intense focus had trapped her, called her, just as he did now.

Up close, barely a foot away, he made her feel bare, exposed. She'd never minded dressing sexy on stage but somehow with his dark gaze scrutinizing her, a slow inspection from head to toe, she knew he disapproved.

His censure was nearly as heavy as her guitar case hanging from her shoulder.

"A drink?" she repeated, trying to force her brain to function despite the rather mad thought that if she ever belonged to a man, it wouldn't be to someone like this, someone so over-whelmingly male, so fiercely controlled.

She wanted ease. Charm. She wanted comfortable.

He wasn't comfortable.

"As in a beverage," he answered almost gently, smiling a little and yet the smile remained at his lips, failed to warm his eyes. Instead his dark eyes burned, his dark eyes owned her, possessed her, a hard sexual possession that had nothing to do with civilized behavior and everything to do with bodies. Skin. *Her* skin.

She felt a cool silvery shiver shoot down her spine, and her body reacted—hair at her nape lifting, goose bumps prickling her arms, even her breasts firmed, nipples peaking.

Joelle pressed her guitar case closer to her hip, making it the latest in body armor. "I understand the concept. We have beverages in America, too," she said, letting him know she understood he was foreign, and yet he couldn't intimidate her.

But she was wary. Not because he posed a physical threat, but because he was different, and she'd always been fascinated by that which was unusual. Intriguing. And he was certainly intriguing.

Tall, darkly handsome and probably very Italian. His accent sounded Italian.

"Then you'll join me," he said, indicating his table.

His stunning confidence dazzled her. "I...I've...plans." Laundry. And packing. She needed to get ready to return home.

"Change them."

There was something...raw...about him, something male and stunningly primitive which didn't go with his superbly tailored suit, the sleek lapel just so, jacket molded, shaping the shoulders and chest, the trousers hanging perfectly, the cuffs hitting the top of his shoe. She'd dated a number of men in the past year and none had been like him. "I can't."

His brow furrowed, his expression hardening. "You must," he said, his tone deceptively soft. "It's important."

Important how? Important to whom?

"Did someone send you?" she asked, looking up into his dark eyes, and once she did, she couldn't look away. He virtually commanded attention, and as she stared at him, she felt the oddest prickle beneath her skin again. More awareness. More unease.

"No."

Her insides tightened. The prickle spread, tingling from her nape to the small of her spine. She didn't know him, did she?

Joelle shook her head, trying to break the strange weave of tension because something *was* happening here and she didn't like it. Her body felt funny. Her chest constricted. She couldn't seem to breathe right. And yet she still couldn't look away.

He knew it, too. His straight black brows were flat, his eyes intently watching hers.

"I'm tired. I've been on stage for over two hours—"

"I know. I was here." He hesitated, as if questioning the wisdom in what he'd say next. "You're very good."

Heat surged through her, a dizzying heat that flooded her limbs, scalded her skin. Somehow it was indecent, this man, his effect on her. "Thank you."

"My table's just here," he said, indicating a table not far from the foot of the stage. "Join me."

"I—" She protested but he was walking away, taking a seat at a small scuffed table bare except for a flickering votive candle.

He flagged down the cocktail waitress and ordered a bottle of champagne, very expensive champagne, before looking up and catching her eye.

He smiled, the smile of one who is used to winning.

Bulldozer, she thought, biting down hard. You can't just come here and take over.

Pulse quickening, she headed toward his table, her leather boots echoing on the hardwood floor. "I'm not joining you," she said, reaching his table.

"Yet you're here."

She hated the sardonic lift of his eyebrow. "I don't want you to waste your money."

"It's just money."

She thought of her kingdom, thought of how close it'd come to financial ruin. Thought of her sisters, how they'd both made marriages of convenience to save Melio. Thought of her past year, and how she'd struggled to get by, how she'd taken two jobs just to pay for the essentials. "It's still wasteful."

"Then you better not let it go undrunk."

Her heart thudded hard, so hard she could feel it pound all the way through her just like the bass guitarist notes had earlier. "What do you want?"

The flickering candlelight played off his face, catching the subtle curve of his lips. There was nothing remotely boyish in his chiseled features. He had a man's face, strong, developed features and she felt something stir inside her, her body betraying her.

Her body liked the way he looked at her.

Her body wanted him to continue looking at her.

He studied her now for a long, level moment, considering her, considering his answer. "I think the question should be, Josie d'Ville, what do you want?"

His answer simply accelerated her racing pulse. Fear, fascination, worry, adrenaline surged through her and her muscles tensed. "This isn't about me."

"But of course it's about you." He gestured to the chair opposite him. "I've come a long way to see you." His inflection firmed. "So sit. *Please*."

What did he mean by that?

Who was he? What exactly did he do?

The dreamer in her hoped he was in the music industry. The dreamer prayed he was someone connected. An agent, maybe. Or even better, a record producer.

Or maybe he was a palace spy. One of those nameless, faceless men who shadowed her this past year, because she was sure her two new brothers-in-law wouldn't allow her to leave home unprotected.

The possibilities filled her, overwhelmed her, and Joelle sat slowly, settling her guitar case at her feet. As she pushed her long hair back from her damp brow she reflected on her performance. Usually she settled into her first set, but tonight nothing had felt right. The energy coming from the audience had felt odd. She'd felt prickly…edgy…not at all her self. More than once she'd had to dig inside herself, finding inner reserves, finding calm to collect her restless thoughts.

She'd tried to tell herself the nerves were due to stress, the fact that she was soon to return home, to return to her duties and the upcoming nuptials to the man she'd never met, let alone seen a photograph of, but duty and marriage had never interfered with a performance before. She'd always loved to sing. Loved being in the moody purple and blue lights, loved the rapt audience, loved the deep bass notes humming through her.

No, it wasn't her imminent return to Melio, which put her teeth on edge. And it wasn't even her impending wedding to a prince she didn't even know. It was this man. He'd skewered her earlier with his eyes, making her feel very naked, and very vulnerable and he was doing it still.

"Why the States?" he asked, breaking the taut silence.

Another current of unease shot through her. *The States,* he'd said, not New Orleans, but the *States.* "What do you mean?"

He leaned back in his chair, arms folded across his chest but he wasn't relaxed. She sensed he was battling to control his temper. "Why do this, here? Why not Nashville? New York? Los Angeles?"

She relaxed a little. Don't be paranoid, she told herself. He's not a palace spy. He doesn't know who you are. "New Orleans is famous for its blues and jazz."

"You've no desire to play in Europe?"

Joelle's nerves danced to life again. Europe. Her world. Home of her kingdom, the two jewel-like islands sparkling in the Mediterranean Sea. "New Orleans is…home."

"You were born here then?"

"My mother was." Or close to here, she silently added, sticking with the persona she'd adopted when she'd first arrived. Eleven months ago she'd gone incognito, darkening her light brown hair, adopting a Southern accent, even wearing funky glasses when she wasn't on stage. Princess Joelle was definitely gone. Josie d'Ville had taken her place.

"Is your mother a d'Ville, too?"

Why all the questions, Joelle wondered? Where was he going with this? "Was," she corrected after a moment. "Before she married." *Before she died.*

Unlike her older sisters, Joelle didn't remember her mother or father. Her parents were just vague memories now, out of her life far longer than they'd ever been in it. Of course she'd wondered about them, endlessly, but it was her mother in particular that mystified Joelle.

Her mother, Star, had been a huge talent. A legendary pop singer. And she'd given it all up to marry a foreign prince.

How ironic that Joelle, a princess, would have given up everything—title, country, prince—to have a chance at being Star.

"So Josie d'Ville is your real name?"

Knots formed in her belly. "More or less."

He laughed softly, mockingly, and the sound pulled her in.

He was magnetic. Compelling. And the intensity in his eyes made her skin sting, her mouth dry. He did this, she thought, fighting panic. But how? Why? And what was he thinking when he looked at her like that? When he stared so long and hard, his expression faintly arrogant, not to mention vaguely amused. Curious. It was almost as if he knew her. Claimed her.

Ridiculous.

He didn't know her. And he couldn't know who she really was. She'd been in New Orleans for over eleven months and no one had even come close to guessing her true identity. And yet there was something in his eyes, something purposeful, masterful, that made her feel small and still. A deer caught in headlights.

The knots inside her grew, the tension filling her until she felt absolutely exhausted from the weight of it.

"More or less," he repeated. "Which really means you're lying—"

"Not lying."

"But not being honest."

She'd never been confronted by anyone with his authority. Power. He exuded power. Overwhelming power. "I'm in the public eye. It's vital I protect my privacy."

"Too little," he said, "too late."

The hair on her nape rose. What was he saying? What did he know?

"You remind me of someone," he blithely continued, "someone in Europe—"

"I have that kind of face. People always think I look like someone they know." Her smile couldn't have been more forced.

"But *you're* not American, are you?"

"My mother—"

"Was American, yes, you've said that." He watched her. Waiting. He knew she was on edge, knew she felt cornered. "How does that explain your French accent then?"

"I don't have a—"

"You do. Beneath the Southern accent there's a very French inflection. It's not always pronounced. I only hear it when you speak quickly. When you're upset."

And he was doing a damn good job of upsetting her, too.

Anxiety rippled through Joelle in waves. "You've a good ear," she answered lightly, even as the panic grew. He didn't know who she was. He couldn't know. He mustn't know. Only a day left, she reminded herself, one day and she'd be on the plane home...

Joelle took a breath, steadied her nerves. There's nothing to fear, she told herself. She knew the bodyguards were out there somewhere, knew she wasn't really alone. "You're right. I did grow up speaking French. My mother's family is from Louisiana. Cajun."

"Cajun?"

"The d'Villes still live just outside Baton Rouge."

"But you weren't raised on the Bayou?"

His words conjured up the wandering Mississippi, the river wide, muddy, the bends ever curving, changing. The great plantations lining the banks, the scattered bayou towns, mostly poor.

It was then Joelle relaxed, the fear easing, turning to something deeper, and far more powerful. He had no idea who she was, what she was. He—like the rest of the world—would never know what she needed, or what she was giving up when she returned home to marry her prince Luigi.

Resentment surged through her. "You're right again." She looked at him hard, fiercely, feeling so much suddenly, feeling the intense pressure and scrutiny she'd been under her entire life. How could he ever know what it'd been like to be little Joelle Ducasse, the orphaned princess? How could he know what it was like to want the world and know you'd only ever get a little island country?

"No, I wasn't raised on the Bayou. But being Cajun isn't about living on the river. It's about having the river in your blood, the river beneath your skin."

"And you have that?"

Her eyes met his, held. "I have so much more than you know." And she wasn't talking about things—possessions—but imagination, hope, and dreams. She'd always had such big dreams.

Silence followed, a long gritty silence that felt like fingernails scraping down a chalkboard and Joelle wished she'd said nothing. Kept her fury and fire to herself. It was none of his business. No one's business. She didn't even know what she was still doing here.

Abruptly she leaned forward, long hair tumbling past her shoulders. "Who are you anyway?"

"Leonardo Marciano Fortino."

She stared at him a long moment, silently repeating the name. He'd spoken his name slowly, carefully, as if imprinting it on her brain, but it meant nothing to her. "Leonardo Marciano Fortino," she repeated. "Quite a mouthful, isn't it?"

Prince Leo Marciano Fortino, of the house of Borgarde, sat back in his chair. She didn't know.

It was worse than he thought, worse than he'd expected…and he'd been prepared for the worst. Not only did his fiancée *not* recognize him, she didn't even know his name.

"Where are you from, Signor Fortino?" Joelle asked, stirring in her seat, fingers flexing ever so slightly.

"Leo," he corrected, biting back a sigh. It was obvious she wasn't ready to settle down, nor was she prepared for the rigors of married life. She was still so young, too young, and he should have listened to his instincts. Her age had troubled him from the start but the palace officials had insisted she was mature for her age. All she needs is a year, they'd said, just give her a year… "Family and friends always call me Leo," he added. "You should, too."

"Yes, but I—"

"Shall call me Leo," he interrupted. "And I've never actually lived in Italy."

"No?"

He saw a flicker of curiosity in her blue-green eyes, and the blue green reminded him of the dazzling Mediterranean waters surrounding her island kingdom. Her eyes hinted at innocence, inexperience, and yet the rest of her exuded sex.

Who was the real Joelle Ducasse?

"Josie." A man approached the table, stopped in front of Joelle. Leo was immediately on guard but Joelle looked completely at ease, and it blew his mind that Joelle lacked proper reserve, lacked any sense of self-preservation.

"You're amazing," the stranger said, standing in front of her, shoving his hands into his pockets. "You're unreal."

"Thank you." Joelle smiled up at the stranger. "That's very kind of you."

"Not kind, honest. I've been here every night you've sung this week, and I've never heard…seen…anyone like you."

Leo felt his gut burn as Joelle's smile dimpled. "What's your name?" she asked.

"Jack."

Leo Borgade remembered the rapt faces in the audience; saw that same combination of lust and longing in Jack's face. Joelle was a bluesy singer, part gospel, part R&B, a little jazz in there, a throaty edge that spoke of big dreams, lots of woes, and the promise of something better coming tomorrow.

Slender, and yet sultry, with long dark hair, lashes so thick and black they made her look both hungry and sleepy at the same time all made her part of the hot steamy New Orleans night. Sexy. Seductive. Mysterious.

No wonder the Jacks of the world wanted her bad.

Leo's lips curved but he wasn't smiling. He was livid. Beyond livid. There was going to be hell to pay.

"Thanks, Jack," Leo said, standing, strategically placing himself between Jack and Joelle. It was a physical gesture. Nothing short of territorial. "It's always nice to hear good things about our Josie. Goodbye. Have a nice night."

Jack nodded dejectedly, and with a wistful look back at Josie, he walked away.

"Our Josie?" Joelle choked.

Leo sat down, shot her a side-glance, and saw she was sputtering mad. Good. Let her wise up. Time she opened her eyes, recognized she was in trouble.

"How could you do that?" she demanded, seething, practically jumping out of her chair, the dim lights overhead casting a sheen on her black leather pants.

"He was drunk."

"He was *nice*."

Leo glanced over his shoulder, caught sight of Jack stumbling out of the bar. "You don't know the meaning of nice, *bambina*."

"It's Josie, not *bambina*, Signor Fortino, and I find your attitude patronizing as well as chauvinistic."

Her Italian accent was flawless. Her temper hot. But she didn't have the right to be angry. She hadn't been deceived. She hadn't been played.

He'd never forget his shock when she strutted onto the stage tonight in her tiny beaded top, low-waisted leather pants, and outrageous stiletto heeled boots. She'd been introduced as Josie—Josie like the name of the kids cartoon Josie and the Pussycats—but this Josie, *his* Joelle, didn't look anything like a kid's cartoon program.

Her face was pale, oval, and luminous in the dark blue gel spotlight. The band members surrounding her were shadowy figures, and in her black beaded cropped top, her tight, black, leather pants and her impossibly high black boots, Josie disappeared in and out of the shadows, with just her pale face and the slim pale patch of midriff reflecting light.

Narrow hips grinding in tight black leather, her breasts pushed up in the tiny top, Princess Joelle Ducasse held the microphone close to her mouth like a long lost lover. And all he could think was, *this is not my fiancée.*

*This can't be my fiancée.*

Even now it blew his mind. His twenty-two-year-old fiancée was a nightclub singer. She'd spent the last year performing off Bourbon Street in this sleazy little place called Club Bleu.

"I don't want to see you hurt," he said roughly, trying to forget her opening act, trying to forget the way she'd strutted onto the stage.

It wasn't a striptease act but it'd come damn close.

"Why do you even care?" she shot back. "You know nothing about me."

"True."

"And Jack was just being friendly."

"Wild dogs can be friendly."

Her cheeks flamed with color but she eyed him steadily. "You know, you're the one who isn't nice. You're pushy. Domineering. Arrogant—"

"Because I'm honest?" Her directness surprised him. She was far from the sweet, retiring princess he'd been promised.

"Because you're rude. Jack was just paying me a compliment—"

"And you need these compliments?" he asked incredulously, seeing too clearly how at the end of the first set, Joelle had slid to her knees only to slither to the edge of the stage. He'd felt the collective groan of the male dominated audience as she fixed her intense blue-green eyes on the audience, her long dark hair spilling over bare shoulders, her skin gleaming with perspiration.

Every man had wanted her. Every man ached for her.

And he'd understood. She looked sexual. Primal.

"What I need is none of your concern," she snapped, voice husky, breaking.

*Wrong,* he answered silently, unable to look away from the fire in her blue-green eyes, like late afternoon sun glinting off the Mediterranean. *You are mine, and what you need concerns me in every way possible.*

Tonight, despite his shock, despite his anger at being deceived by King Remi and the Melio palace handlers, he wanted her in the purest, rawest sense of the word. Wanted her to take. To possess. To own. Because she was his.

Physical desire hadn't been part of the equation when he agreed to marry the youngest Ducasse. It'd been business. He was a titled prince without a kingdom, and she was a princess with a kingdom in need of heirs. Together they'd be fruitful and multiply. He'd have his kingdom and children, Melio would have their king and next generation, Joelle would fulfill her destiny.

*Or would she?*

The cocktail waitress arrived with the champagne bottle and two freshly washed flutes.

Joelle didn't even look at the waitress, her head turned, her gaze averted. He realized she was fighting hard to control her temper.

The waitress popped the cork but still Joelle refused to make eye contact.

He had no patience for theatrics. He was the one that should be angry, not her. Six weeks ago he'd heard the rumors about the Princess Ducasse look-alike in New Orleans. He'd heard rumors that the singer had a voice that could break hearts and a face to match.

More curious than concerned, he'd contacted the Melio palace, and they'd said they'd heard the rumors, too. But it couldn't be true, they told him. Joelle, he was assured, was safe in Europe, immersed in her studies at an exclusive music conservatory, eagerly planning her wedding.

*Eagerly planning her wedding.*

Indeed. She was the epitome of the blushing bride.

"I was protecting you," he said at last, exasperated by her stubborn silence.

"I don't need your protection," she answered tartly as the waitress filled their flutes, the pale gold champagne bubbling out fast, sending white foam spilling over the delicate glass rims.

He waited for the waitress to leave. "You're naïve."

"You're Italian."

"And that's a problem?"

"Yes."

He sat silent a moment studying her. "Why?"

He looked at her so hard Joelle shivered on the inside. There was something intense in his gaze, something that reached into her and held her still.

She didn't dislike him. She was just terrified of him. Of her response to him. He made her feel painfully self-conscious, far too aware of herself. Far too aware of him.

"And what are your issues with Italian men, *bambina?*"

# CHAPTER TWO

HER issues...

Joelle swallowed, shifted. *What were those issues?* Suddenly she couldn't think of anything but how she felt. Because she felt wild, as if there was only chaos on the inside and her skin could barely hold it all in.

She was humming right now, her body literally zinging with nervous energy. It crossed her mind that everything she was afraid of, everything she feared, was everything she'd wanted to know.

Like sex. She wanted to know all about sex. She wanted to live it, feel it, understand it. She wanted to be part of the world before she was locked away in Melio's ivory tower.

"I'm waiting," he said.

But not patiently, she thought, all fire on the inside, an incredible roar of flame and heat. He was doing this to her. He was making her feel hot, irritable, explosive.

He was making her think of all the things she didn't know. Ignition, conflagration, combustion. She felt a tremor course through her. "Italian men are...difficult."

"How so?"

His voice wrapped around her skin, warm, discomfiting. "They're demanding."

"As they should be."

This was madness, she thought, alarm sounding in the back of her brain. You should be home finishing your packing. You should get up and go now. You should be anywhere but sitting here, with him.

But she couldn't move, couldn't look away. Leo Fortino was different from the men she knew, different from anyone she'd ever met. He was thrilling in a heart-stopping kind of way. Thrilling like dancing on the mouth of a volcano. "Possessive."

"A virtue."

"Proud."

Leo lifted a flute, held it out to her, the gold liquid shimmering in the votive's flickering light. "Without a doubt."

She hesitated before taking the glass. And once she took the flute, he flashed her a shadow of a smile, looking every bit the predator. Then he lifted his own flute in a toast. "And you're wise to remember that, *bambina*."

*Bambina*. Baby. Child. But she wasn't a child. And that's exactly what no one in Europe, in Melio, seemed to realize. She might only be twenty-two, but on the inside she was old.

On the inside she was wise. She'd known all along there'd be just this year—one brief year—to pull herself together, to come to grips with Grandmama's death, her Grandpapa's expectations. The past eleven months and odd weeks had been good for her, too. She was stronger. More determined. She'd do what needed to be done. Once she returned. But she hadn't returned yet.

She had one more day of freedom left. One more night of being Josie, not Joelle, of being a woman, not a princess.

"Cheers," he said, lightly clinking his glass against hers.

Glancing across at dark, sexy Leo Fortino, Joelle couldn't help wondering if she still had time to find that romance to last a lifetime, a romance that would carry her through years of cordial marital relations, but relations lacking fire and ice.

And she wanted fire. She wanted sex. Passion.

"Cheers," she whispered, lifting the flute to her lips, knowing Grandmama would be turning over in her grave.

Grandmama had always been so determined to see her granddaughters instilled with the good morals, values and integrity she said the modern young nobles lacked today.

Grandmama said that the new generation didn't understand that to lead, one must sacrifice, and that being able to serve one's country was the greatest of all honors.

*I'm sorry, Grandmama,* Joelle thought, tipping the flute, *but I need tonight. I need something so hot, so intense I'll remember it forever. I need something that's mine, all mine, something that can't ever be taken from me.*

The champagne tasted cold and fizzed across her tongue and yet when she swallowed it was hot going down.

She could hear Grandmama *cluck-clucking* in the back of her head, preparing to warn her yet again about the dangers of being curious, the dangers of wanting to know everything. *Only foolish women play with fire,* Grandmama used to say, *and don't forget what curiosity did to that poor little cat...*

Carefully she set the glass down, and as she returned the flute to the table, Leo reached out to take her left hand in his.

She shivered at the touch. His gaze lifted, he looked up into her eyes and then back down at her hand. For a long moment he simply inspected her bare fingers.

"No ring?" he asked at last, holding her hand firmly, her palm brushing his, his fingers wrapped around hers.

Heat exploded inside her at the prolonged contact. "I'm not married."

Again he looked up into her eyes. "Surely you're spoken for?"

Joelle hated the sharp nibble of guilt, the bite on her conscience. She knew she'd never be able to sit here, do this, if she could picture Prince Luigi's face, know him as a real person. As it was, Luigi seemed fictional, like a figment of her imagination. Mysterious wealthy prince agrees to marry poor princess...

But why hadn't her prince ever tried to meet her? Why had he cared so little about her? He'd been to Melio. He'd inspected his future kingdom, checked out his future holdings, looked at the ports, the palace, the smaller island of Mejia, but he'd never bothered to even introduce himself to her.

He'd never bothered with her at all.

Hurt, ashamed, Joelle burned hot, then cold. "I'm not much for jewelry."

Leo made a rough sound in the back of his throat, his fingers closing more firmly around hers. "You're not dating, are you?"

Her sense of self-preservation told her to be careful, very careful. She saw the intensity in his expression, the flame in his eyes. He was angry. But why? Joelle swallowed, struggled to speak around the lump filling her throat. "I do go out, yes."

He released her hand and she quickly made a fist, trying to forget how his touch had jolted through her, sharp and hot like the lick of a flame. How could such an impersonal touch, the simple clasping of fingers, make her feel this, or so raw and exposed?

How could the touch of his hand make her want more heat, more sensation, more skin?

Maybe…maybe he could be…

She lifted her head, looked into his face. Their gazes locked and she saw something in his eyes that filled her with fresh heat.

He wanted her.

He claimed her.

But that was crazy. Absurd. She shifted yet again, her tongue sticking to the roof of her mouth. Maybe he was the one. The one who'd take her virginity, give her experience, allowing her to go to her wedding as a woman of the world rather than a sheltered, incompetent, *ignorant* bride.

She'd been waiting for the right man, wanting a sophisticated, intelligent partner, one that would make a satisfying lover. But she'd been picky, too picky, and she was out of time. With the wedding three weeks away, and Grandfather's birthday seven days from today, she needed to act fast. Or accept the fact that she'd marry her Prince Borgarde without knowing what she needed to know. Sex, quite frankly, puzzled her. The mechanics were clear, but the intimacy—the naked body on naked body—unnerved her.

She struggled to find words, to put together a coherent sentence, one that she could actually speak out loud, but her mouth was so dry, her throat felt scratchy and she lifted the flute, took a sip of the tart sweet champagne.

"So what am I doing here?" she asked faintly, clutching the stem of the flute. "What am I doing sitting with you?"

His eyes never left her mouth. "Answering your curiosity, I imagine."

He had the most piercing gaze, a gaze that made her feel young and inexperienced, a gaze that made her want to find a big comfy sweatshirt and pull it over her head, hiding her hips and breasts…

For a moment she forgot what they were discussing, or where they were. For a moment she couldn't think, too swamped by the sudden heat in her veins and the slow, heavy pounding of her heart.

For a moment there was no one else. No one in the club. No one at the exit. No one at the bar.

And looking at him, she was lost. There was just him, Leo Marciano Fortino, a man with dark eyes that held her fast, that let her know what he wanted, and he wanted her, body and soul.

Then slowly it came back to her, what he'd said, what they'd been discussing. Her curiosity.

He was right. She was curious. She'd always had a problem being so curious, wanting to know so much, wanting to know virtually everything.

When she was growing up Grandmother Astrid was always scolding her about going too far, asking for too much. *Never forget, cherie,* Grandmama would lecture, *curiosity killed the cat. Don't let it kill you.*

But the way things were going curiosity might very well be the end of her. Right now she felt like a dumb moth fascinated by flame. "I do have an insatiable curiosity."

His mouth quirked, a curving that revealed the full sensuality of his lower lip. "And you're curious about me?"

She nodded. She couldn't speak.

His gaze shifted from her face to her tightly closed fist. "Can I offer you one bit of advice, *bambina?*"

Again she nodded.

"You need to be more careful," he said.

Icy heat shivered up and down Joelle's spine. This is dangerous, a little voice whispered inside her. It's one thing to want experience, it's another to get involved. "But I am careful."

She could tell he wasn't convinced.

"There are a lot of men who'd take advantage of your curious nature," he added.

Immediately blood surged through her, flooding her face, melting the bones of her hips and knees. Embarrassed, she looked away, breaking his intense hold.

Leo knocked her off balance, and her brain was no longer in

gear, her body too alive. She was finding it harder and harder to think clearly.

She'd known for years that life was dog-eat-dog. Fierce. Hard. Possibly ugly. Life was Darwinian theory at its best. Survival of the fittest. Only the strong survive.

And that's how she'd tried to live. But she didn't feel strong now. She felt confused. Emotional.

She should have never agreed to an arranged marriage but it was too late to cancel, too late to disappoint Grandfather, the people of Melio, her fiancé and his family. They were counting on a lavish wedding. A properly enthusiastic bride. Somewhere, somehow, she'd have to find the eager expectancy.

Or at the very least, serenity.

Unfortunately the closer it came to the wedding, the less serene she felt. It was bad enough marrying a man she didn't know, a man who didn't care to know her, a man she wouldn't even recognize on the street, but to marry such a man without knowing anything about *sex?*

And that was the real issue. She didn't want to walk down the aisle a virgin. Prince Borgade needed a wife. She didn't have to be inexperienced. The prince was getting her country. He didn't need her virginity.

All her life she'd wanted to be like her sister, Nicolette. Bold. Confident. Brazen. Instead she was more like Chantal. Proud. Shy. Rather reserved.

But shyness didn't excuse ignorance, and she absolutely refused to go to bed with a man—even her husband—without knowing anything. She couldn't bear to think that in three weeks she'd strip off her wedding gown and climb into bed with a husband she'd only just met and lie there naked and wait for God knows what.

The God knows what part really got to her.

There was no way she wanted to feel foolish on her wedding night. There was no way she wanted to be intimidated. Far better to know what to expect. To understand the sequence of events…the sensation…the emotion.

And again the thought hit her— Leo could teach her. She was a fast learner. She really only needed just one night.

Abruptly she reached for her flute, downed the rest of her champagne. The heat and bubbles made her eyes burn. Her stomach lurched a little at the hit of alcohol. "I should eat something." She frowned at her empty glass. "The bubbles are going straight to my head."

"You haven't had dinner?"

"I usually don't eat until after the show wraps. Can't eat before. Too much adrenaline."

There was the briefest hesitation before Leo reached into his wallet, drew out a couple hundred-dollar bills and left them on the table. "If we leave now we could still make it to Brennan's before they close."

Brennan's—the famous Brennan's where food was fabulous and the French Quarter atmosphere perfect—was just around the corner and had practically become an institution. "You're inviting me to dinner?"

His dark eyes met hers. "You wanted me to."

True. No point in arguing that.

Joelle swallowed, her throat scratchy dry, rough from the champagne, the smoky club and too much singing. But her scratchy throat was nothing compared to the frantic tempo of her pulse. "Let me just change."

Behind the bar, in the small bathroom with the bare lightbulb, Joelle took a paper towel and blotted her face, before taking a Q-tip and makeup remover to lighten some of the stark black eyeliner from around her eyes.

You're sure you want to do this? she asked her reflection, her stomach a ball of nerves. But Joelle already knew the answer to that. Yes. She wanted to do this. Badly.

Leo rose as Joelle emerged from the back of the club. She'd taken some of the heavier eye makeup off and changed into jeans and a long gauzy cream blouse with a lace edged neckline. In her jeans and peasant style blouse she looked even younger than before. And just like that his gut tightened, his body jerking to life, his groin hard, his temper nearly as hot.

Nothing, he thought with a flash of painful insight, would ever be the same for either of them again.

Joelle felt Leo watching her as she approached the table, and slowly, reluctantly she met his speculative gaze.

As his eyes met hers, she felt a funny rush in her middle, the same crazy adrenaline she experienced when on stage, like one of those nights when she wore a micromini skirt paired with thigh high boots.

She felt Leo's narrowed gaze slowly inspect her and she saw herself through his eyes, saw her long loose hair, saw the simple blouse, the tight faded jeans, the open-toed sandals.

"Do you know what you're doing, Josie?" he said at last.

The air bottled in her lungs and she felt her legs wobble. Then she deliberately exhaled and forced a smile. "I certainly hope so."

They left the club, stepping out into the warm humid night of early June and Joelle drew a deep breath, immediately relaxing.

She loved New Orleans, had loved her year in the States. But most of all, she'd loved being real.

Joelle didn't remember when she'd begun to chafe at the royal life, but sometime in the last several years—as both sisters left—she'd grown to hate her life…the structure and routine.

She hated the gowns and gloves, the endless smiling for visiting dignitaries. Hated the formalities, the stiff royal receptions, the lengthy public functions. Chantal was good at shaking hands and kissing babies. Nicolette—smart, witty—was the speechmaker supreme. But Joelle had always found the public attention, the constant demands difficult, but after Grandmama died the burden had become intolerable.

She missed Grandmama so much she couldn't bear to get out of bed, couldn't bear to face people, couldn't bear to smile her tight professional princess smile.

How could she smile when she'd lost the one person who loved her no matter what? How could she smile when she'd lost the person who held her and comforted her all those years after Mother and Father died?

Grandmama was the only one who knew how much Joelle struggled with the pressures of royal life. Grandmama was the only one who knew that Joelle still grieved for her missing parents. Grandmama was the only one who knew that deep down Joelle still hoped, strange and impossible as it was, to someday bump into her mother and her father, to find them strolling down the street, to be reunited with the past she so desperately missed.

The emotion rose up, huge, hot, overpowering.

Grandmama knew Joelle's need to love, and be loved, and she never ridiculed her, never made her feel less, never made her feel anything but good. And generous. And kind.

And now Grandmama was gone and Joelle had to grow up and tomorrow she'd be on the plane home, back to Melio. Back to duty. Back to responsibility.

And she'd do it. She'd do it because Nicolette had shouldered the duties just as Chantal had, and Joelle was determined to do her part now, too. For Grandmama and Grandpapa, if nothing else.

Joelle drew a breath, listened to their footsteps echoing off the pavement as they walked in silence. Brennan's was just ahead, a block away and the quarter-moon gave off dim light.

Tomorrow night she'd be home. A week from now would be Grandpapa's eighty-fifth birthday party. And then in three weeks the wedding. Three weeks and she'd be Her Royal Highness, Princess Ducasse Borgarde.

"That's the second heavy sigh," Leo said, before abruptly shoving his arm out in front of her, stopping her at the curb. A taxi whizzed by, virtually flying through the intersection, bumping over the corner's cobblestones.

Joelle shuddered inwardly as Leo's arm pressed against her chest, the sleeve of his elegant suit rubbing at the thin cotton of her blouse.

"I was thinking," she said, pushing away from the arm, discomfited by the gesture. He'd put his arm out as if she were a impulsive child, just as he'd called her *bambina* earlier.

His arm dropped. He gazed down at her, brows furrowed. "You're reckless."

"I'm not. I know what I'm doing. I walk home every night, and I know this city—"

"You walk home every night?"

"After I finish at Club Bleu."

''Where do you live?''

''Six, seven blocks from here.''

''And you walk? Alone?''

Disapproval sharpened his tone, a disapproval so reminiscent of the censure she'd found in Melio when she balked at attending one more luncheon, one more ribbon cutting, that Joelle stopped midstep, anger rifling through her. ''Since you disapprove of virtually everything I say or do, why *are* you taking me to dinner?''

The old-fashioned street lamps shone down on them, silhouetting Leo's height, casting dim yellow light on his profile. He looked hard, proud...*Roman.* ''I'm trying to understand you.''

''What's there to understand? I'm twenty-two, successful, independent. I do what I want, go where I want, make my own decisions.''

''Even though it puts you in danger?''

''I'm not in danger.''

He shook his head in mute frustration. ''How do you know? How do you know *I'm* not dangerous?''

A tremor shot through her. Good question, she thought. She didn't.

Or did she?

She stared up at him, brow creased, studying his hard features. All right. He did scare her. But he didn't strike her as violent. Controlling, yes, but cruel, no. ''You wouldn't hurt me,'' she said at last, burying her hands in her jean pockets. ''You're not that kind of a man.''

He muttered something in Italian she couldn't completely hear, but she did catch a couple choice swear words along with a very cryptic, ''You don't know.''

They were walking again and crossed to Royal Street. Brennan's came into view, the exterior painted the softest shade of pink.

Leo held the dark green door open for her and as Joelle moved past him she felt a current of awareness shoot through her, her body prickling from head to toe, her skin painfully sensitive.

She shot him a cautious glance, wondering yet again how he had this effect on her. Yes, he was tall. Yes, he exuded strength.

But it wasn't the physical size of him as much as the energy coming from within.

Leo Fortino would be formidable if crossed.

The hostess seated them almost immediately, upstairs in one of the smaller dining rooms, this one painted a rich dark red, the tall French windows overlooking the lush interior courtyard.

The kitchen would be closing within the hour and after giving the menu a quick perusal, they both ordered.

The soup, Louisiana Crab Bisque, arrived quickly and Joelle, who'd thought she was hungry, could barely get her spoon to her mouth.

It was one thing to find a man heart-stoppingly attractive. It was another to eat sitting across from him.

Leo noticed she'd barely touched her soup. His dark gaze rested on her face. "You don't prefer it?"

Oh, there went the butterflies in her stomach again. When he looked at her like that, so directly, so intently, she felt as if she were lost. Completely. Totally.

"I do. It's delicious," she said, forcing the spoon up to her lips and choking the mouthful down.

But she had his full attention now and the next sip was even harder than the last.

"So what's wrong?"

She pushed back a heavy wave of hair, wishing she'd thought to tie it back but it was too late for that. Just as it was too late to duck out of dinner. Dining at Brennan's with Leo had sounded exciting when she was still at Club Bleu, but now that they were here, seated in a virtually empty dining room, the dark red walls warm and intimate, she was finding the flurry of nerves too much.

"How old are you?" she asked suddenly, setting her spoon down.

"Thirty-two."

Wow. She exhaled slowly, turning into a massive ball of insecurity. He was ten years older than her. Ten years. Imagine the wealth of knowledge he had…especially when it came to women. "When's your birthday?"

"May 4."

A month ago today. She smiled faintly, thinking that his birth date explained a lot "You're a Taurus."

"A Taurus?"

"You know…astrology…the sun signs."

He gestured dismissively. "I don't follow any of that."

The gesture, coupled with his patronizing tone, rankled her. On one hand he was a gorgeous male, but on the other he was hopelessly arrogant. "You don't have to follow anything. It is what it is. It exists even if you don't believe in it."

"But you do?" he persisted, indicating to the waiter that the soup dishes could be cleared.

"It's fun."

Leo's jaw flexed and Joelle felt a tingly shiver run through her. Leo didn't approve.

"It's stupidity."

She blinked, trying to clear the haze of red before her eyes. "How can you do that? How can you be so judgmental?"

"Because you're supposed to be an intelligent woman. You're supposed to think for yourself, not buy into all that New Age stuff. Astrology, sun signs, crystals, palm reading, aura reading—"

"Excuse me, but I never said I was into New Age mysticism. I never brought up crystals or aura readings. I just asked you when your birthday was, and when you told me, I said, you're a Taurus. That was it." What was going on here? Why was she getting such mixed signals?

He'd sought her out earlier. He'd watched her tonight, approached her after the set ended, asked her to join him for a drink. Why?

"You know, Leo, I know you don't approve of me, and I don't know why. Maybe it's because I don't understand what, or who, you think I am. But I'm not a druggie. I don't smoke, inhale, pop pills. I don't drink much. I'm not covered in multiple piercings and body tattoos. I just like to sing." She looked up at him, her gaze meeting his. "And I love to entertain."

As she spoke, her long dark hair fell forward, her right hand fisted on the table, and her voice dropped, deepening with a husky sensuality and fury.

Joelle's gaze held his. "Obviously there are a lot of things you don't like about me. Is there anything you do?"

*Is there anything he did?*

Leo felt his body respond at the provocative question, and leaning back in his chair he took in her small taunting smile, the cool anger in her blue-green eyes. "Your eyes," he said bluntly. She had beautiful eyes, the lashes so thick and long, even more dramatic now with the extra set of false lashes at the outer corners.

"Your hair." His gaze touched her hair, the incredible length, the rich color. He'd love to tangle his hands in her hair, feel the glossy weight.

"Your mouth," he added, staring at her mouth and watching her bite into her lower lip, chewing on the tender skin. Her lips were full, soft and painted a pale pinky-beige. Her lips were the color of skin, making him think nude, naked, wicked.

He watched her chew on that soft lower lip and felt the silence between them lengthen, felt the tension mount.

She was squirming from the tension. He saw the desire in the darkening of her eyes, the flush in her cheeks, her restlessness at the table.

Would she go to bed with him? Would she sleep with him—a stranger—three weeks before her wedding? "Your body." He felt harsh, cruel, but he needed information. There was so much he didn't know, so much about her he didn't understand.

"And that's all you like about me?" she asked, her voice faint, almost tremulous, in the rich dark red dining room. "Lips, hair, body?"

His chest grew tight, his groin hot and hard. Things were getting complicated. How much did he say? How much did he give away?

He knew his silence hurt her. He saw her smooth throat work, saw her hand tremble as she sorted out her silverware on the linen tablecloth. She was fighting for control, fighting to be calm.

And yet he remained silent, thinking, weighing, deliberating. He sorted through his actions, reactions, examined his motivations.

If he told her who he was, she'd change before his eyes. He

knew she'd hide herself, the true self and become Princess Ducasse. But he didn't want a part. He wanted the real thing.

He wanted to know *her*. Wanted the good, the bad, the ugly.

It was truth he needed now. Truth to cut through the lies and pretense. Truth so he'd know whom he was marrying.

Or if he should even marry her.

But the question of marriage, of suitability of marriage, did nothing to dampen his hunger. He wanted her. His body ached. His trousers cut him.

She was supposed to be innocent.

He was supposed to be the good prince.

Tragically, nothing was as it should be.

"No," he said softly, eyes holding her, eyes taking her, eyes letting her know what he'd do given the opportunity, "I don't just want your body. I want your mind, too."

# CHAPTER THREE

JOELLE jerked at the rawness of Leo's answer. He had a hard voice, a decisive voice, and when he said he wanted her—not just her body, but also her mind—she felt as if he'd launched an assault...

Crossbows, battleaxes, and all.

Mouth dry, she stared across at him. And looking into his eyes was yet another mistake in a night of mistakes.

She'd never looked this closely into a man's face before, never let herself look so intimately into someone's eyes, and it wasn't just intimate, it was excruciating.

His eyes were dark, but not brown as she'd thought, but a deep dark green, like the olives of Tuscany, the color of the woods in Melio where sunlight fell in slender streaks between fragrant pine branches.

Cool. Warm. Intelligent. Beautiful.

She felt her lips nearly curve in appreciation, and then small muscles creased at the corner of his eyes and she felt all air leave her body.

The table was too small. They were sitting far too close. Leo was too big.

She shivered all the way through and drew a rough, uncomfortable breath causing the skin on her nape to tingle. The goose bumps returned, this time covering every inch of skin, tightening even her breasts, causing her nipples to peak against the soft contour of her silk bra.

It was a strange response, and such a strong one, too.

Leo shifted and his knee brushed hers beneath the table. Joelle gasped at the sharp heat shooting through her. Beneath the table she pressed her knees together, pressing the muscles of her inner thighs tight, trying to deny the flood of want.

The flood of need.

He'd turned her on from the very first look, and now she was melting on the inside, melting because of him. Just one touch and she tensed, body hot, aching. Damp.

Glancing up, she met Leo's gaze once again. His features were still beautiful but not quite so hard and she didn't know if it was the hidden warmth in his eyes or the fact that his mouth had gentled, accenting his chin, flat across the bottom with a hint of a cleft, but she wanted to kiss him. Felt almost desperate to feel his mouth against hers.

There was so much she didn't know. So much she wanted to understand. Like how a man's lips could stir her imagination and how his breath would feel blowing lightly, tormentingly against her skin...

"You want my mind?" she whispered, thinking, wishing it were so. No one had ever wanted her mind. No one had ever wanted to know her.

"Is that such a bad thing?"

She couldn't help it. She felt her lips curve up, into a wide rueful smile. "They say the best sex starts with the brain."

Leo smiled, but it was different than hers. It wasn't a warm smile, or wry or remotely rueful. No, his smile wasn't one of amusement. Instead he looked as if he were about to declare war.

Joelle went weak in the middle, and the weakness seeped through her limbs. Thank God she was sitting otherwise she would have come crashing down.

Leo's smile faded. "Indeed. The brain is the primary sexual organ. Engage the brain for ultimate pleasure."

She blushed, not just from his words, but the intentness of his gaze. She felt even more aware of him than before. Her heart hammered harder. Her mouth went dry. Muscles clenched deep inside of her.

Joelle felt so hot, so wound up. Eleven months here and she'd never felt anything like this. But the sensations surging through her, the emotions rocking her, weren't gentle, weren't playful, weren't fun.

This was sexual. Brutal.

Fire and ice, she whispered. This is what you thought you wanted...

"You look thirsty," Leo said, his expression lazy, blatantly sexual, leaning forward to fill her wineglass.

But beneath the sexual implication there was a warm, complex sensuality that reached out to her, beckoned her.

She felt fingers of his sensual warmth creep through her.

She *was* thirsty, she thought. But then, she'd been thirsty for years: thirsty for everything she'd never done, thirsty for experience and wisdom, thirsty for knowledge, thirsty for insight, thirsty to be more Joelle.

Her glass filled, Leo sat back. "Drink."

If only it were that easy. Her nose wrinkled as she picked up her glass and set it down again untouched. She honestly didn't think she could eat or drink anything if she tried. "I don't think I can."

"Why not?"

"Too much adrenaline."

Leo thought she'd been beautiful on stage—sexier than hell in the tight flared leather pants, the stiletto heel boots—but nothing was as sexy as listening to her speak, watching her mouth curve, hearing the words "too much adrenaline" in that smoky voice of hers, a voice shaded with dreams and blues.

He understood adrenaline. At one point in his life he'd lived from one adrenaline surge to another, needing huge physical challenges to focus his endless energy, his restlessness haunting him, chasing him around the globe. But there was something about her, and her admission of nerves and adrenaline that touched him.

"What's bothering you?" he asked, filling his glass.

"You."

He looked up in time to see her blue-green eyes flash. "I'm not."

"You are." She inhaled in a rush. More nerves, he thought.

"You're not like most men I know," she added and she touched the tip of her tongue to her upper lip.

Leo's gut felt as hard as his groin. He gritted his teeth, thinking he'd have to peel his skin off in a minute if his body didn't cool down. "And what are those men like?"

"Charming. Easygoing. Harmless."

"That's me."

Joelle laughed. "You're impossible."

"Perhaps." He suddenly reached out, lightly touched her cheek. Her skin was warm, soft and her head jerked up, eyes wide, wary. "You've a beautiful laugh, *bambina*. You should laugh more."

Joelle blushed, looked away, realized dinner was on the way. The waiters presented the plates with a flourish and left them alone to eat. And Joelle realized she wasn't as nervous as she'd been.

Leo's mood seemed lighter as well, his dark gaze warmer, less shuttered, and she continued to relax, enjoying her entrée, giving in to the pleasure of a well-cooked meal.

And sitting there, across from Leo, in Brennan's upstairs dining room, red walls cocooning them, the French cuisine sublime, she thought this was the kind of evening where even the little things took on a larger than life significance.

The flawless white table linens felt silky smooth beneath her fingers. The candle glowed warmly, reflecting brilliantly off the crystal and china. The glimpse of moon outside the windowpane added to the ambiance.

Joelle held her wine goblet by the stem, the glass bowl huge, round, full, the red wine barely filling the basin as she listened to Leo talk about his life abroad, how he didn't live in one place, but many, with homes in London, Santiago, Chile, Zurich. He considered himself a man of the world instead of a man of one country.

She liked the sound of his voice, the strength in his voice and she knew she was smiling as she listened, her eyes resting on his face, her body leaning ever so slightly forward, her legs crossed beneath the table.

It crossed her mind that this is how she imagined America to be—how life to be—the richness, the complexity, the complicated beauty. No easy answers. No right answer. Just life. Just people. Just energy, sound and motion.

"You've traveled extensively," he said, shifting the focus from his own background to hers. "Where have you felt most at home?

"Here." It was easy to answer. She'd never traveled as much as Leo had, but no place had felt like this.

She'd loved the past eleven and a half months. Loved being no one, a nonentity, invisible on New Orleans's streets.

She'd loved walking the French Quarter late at night, guitar slung over her shoulder, heading back to the little apartment she shared with Lacy from Georgia.

She'd loved waking early, grabbing a beignet and coffee across from St. Charles before all the tourists descended.

There'd been so much to embrace here.

Carnival. The sultry heat wrapping the city in summer. The crumbly red bricks of the old buildings. The stately wrought-iron balconies overhanging narrow streets.

Tipping her wine goblet, Joelle watched the wine swirl. "Everything felt right here. *I* felt right here."

"Are you planning on staying in New Orleans then?" Leo's deep voice, rich and cultured, like gold marble shot with veins of black rushed through her, across her taut senses, stirring something deep inside of her.

"No."

"Why not?"

Looking up, she met his eyes, saw that he was trying to figure out where she was, what she was thinking. No one had ever looked at her so long, listened so intently, and she wondered if she'd ever have this again, after she married. Would she ever sit at a table and feel special? Desirable? Would Luigi even want to listen to her?

Resolutely Joelle pushed thoughts of Luigi out of mind, and shrugged in answer to Leo's question. She focused on the candle on their table, trying to keep the tears from burning. "I have to."

"Why the have to? You're an adult. Do what you want to do."

"It's not that simple." She reached out to the candle, put her hand above the flame, felt the lick of heat. "We all have a purpose...something we're supposed to do."

"So it's work that calls you back?"

"Yes. I've a new job waiting."

''What kind of job?''

She laughed without a trace of humor. ''It's awful. Trust me. You don't want to know.''

''That bad?''

She blinked back sudden stinging tears. ''Worse.''

He stared at her long and hard, his black brows furrowed, and then he muttered something intelligible beneath his breath. He stood abruptly, reached for his wallet. ''It's time we go.''

He was angry. Joelle felt a wobble inside her. What had she said? ''Leo?''

But he wasn't looking at her; he was sliding his wallet back into his coat pocket, now heading for the stairs.

Joelle trailed after him on shaky legs. They exited the entrance, reached the street and Leo set off down Royal Street, opposite the way they came. She glanced at him as they walked, tried to read his expression, but it was dark, his profile granite hard, and all she felt coming off of him was waves of anger.

They walked one block, and then another. The French Quarter wasn't all that big and if they continued the direction they were heading, they'd soon hit Canal Street, exiting the French Quarter.

''Leo?'' she asked uncertainly.

''What?''

''Where…'' She swallowed, gathered her courage. It wasn't as if they hadn't just spent three hours together. ''Where are we going?''

He stopped abruptly beneath a street lamp, turned, and faced her. ''Where do you think we're going?''

She shook her head. She didn't understand the look she saw in his eye. At the moment she didn't understand anything.

There was a long moment of silence, a moment where she saw a frustration in his dark eyes, an emotion that held anger as well as passion. Then he backed her into a dark alcove, the large arched doorway a former carriage entrance like so many in the French Quarter.

''We've had drinks,'' he said flatly.

''Yes.''

''We've had dinner.''

She felt his coat fall open, felt the jacket brush against her breasts. "At Brennan's."

He leaned forward, one arm moved above her head, bracing himself against the door. "We've had coffee. Dessert. Now you tell me what happens next."

Joelle locked her knees. Fear mingled with desire. "I don't know."

"Yes, you do."

It was hard to see his face, the shadows hid his expression but she felt the heat radiating from him, felt the warmth of his body without him touching her.

Leo made her feel awash in emotion, and ever since she met him she was swinging like a pendulum from one emotion to another. She was swinging even now and the sense of momentum, the feeling of being in perpetual motion, in perpetual flux, unnerved her more than she could say.

She blinked back tears, knowing they were tears of fatigue, and stress. It'd been a difficult week, packing, saying her good-byes, but the tears were also a release. She'd been so wound up all night…frazzled by a need she couldn't answer.

But he could.

He could quiet the humming in her veins. He could put out the fire.

She felt him move closer, his head bending down. She held her breath, certain he would kiss her. She wanted the kiss. She feared the kiss.

From the corner of her eye she saw his arm move. His thumb strummed her cheek. Her head spun. She needed air but she didn't dare to breathe.

Leo's eyes were dark, his expression intense. "Tell me."

She opened her mouth, stole a breath, and yet her pulse was slowing, desire—anticipation—washing through her in endless waves.

His thumb dropped to her mouth. Lightly he brushed the pad of his thumb across her lips. Pinpricks of light exploded inside her head. Hot sensation rocketed through her and she tensed, hands, arms, legs, everything.

She wanted, wanted, wanted him. She didn't even know

where to begin, what to ask for. The hunger, the need, was alive inside her and she knew nothing could happen here, in this dark alcove, nothing would happen. Leo Fortino didn't strike her as a man who'd taken a woman on a city sidewalk.

She reached up to touch the collar of his shirt, too afraid to touch his skin and yet needing contact, needing to connect. "We go…"

"Yes?" His thumb was drawing circles on her swollen lower lip. The circles were slowly driving her mad.

She closed her eyes, tried to clear her brain. "We go to your—"

"My?"

"Hotel—"

She'd said what he'd wanted to hear. His head dropped. He silenced the rest with a kiss.

His lips were firm, his breath cool and she stiffened with surprise. She'd kissed before, felt rather proficient in terms of kissing but this wasn't a mere kiss, this was like nothing she'd ever experienced before.

His lips moved across hers, deliberately, thoroughly, a sensual exploration intended to stir her, wake every little nerve ending to life and he succeeded. Too well. Her lower lip quivered, tingled and the tingle shot all the way through her, straight to her belly, which felt hot and tight with need.

But that was only the beginning. His mouth drew the heat from hers and the slow exploration flared into something fierce, demanding.

His hard body pressed against hers, his thighs moved between hers and she felt trapped, skewered, the very way he'd trapped her in his gaze earlier, but this time it was with his body.

She felt the hard planes of his chest crush her breasts, the sinewy shape of his thigh between her own and she groaned as he moved against her, his knee up, between her thighs, creating friction, sensation.

Her groan was like tossing gasoline on a fire.

Leo's hands moved from the wall to her head, his palms sliding through her hair, fingers tightening in her long hair, holding her captive.

His desire was raw. His hunger stunned her. He was so not like anything she understood, so beyond anything she could control, and yet she wanted it all—the passion, the fury, the shiver of fraught nerves. All the while her body was melting, her defenses negligent. She'd known from the beginning she couldn't resist him. She'd known from the very first glance that she'd be his.

She felt one of Leo's hands drop from her hair, to her cheek and her jawbone before sliding down the length of her neck. The path his hand took was as tortuous as it was delicious and Joelle arched helplessly up against Leo's body, her hips meeting his, her head tipping, exposing more, more skin.

She felt Leo's fingertips graze her collarbone; stroke the swell of her breast. Shivery pleasure danced through her. Her lips parted, gasped, as his hand moved beneath the thin blouse to find hot bare skin.

It was her soft indrawn take of air that finally penetrated Leo's brain. He was undressing her here, virtually making love to her here, on the street, in a gloomy alcove littered with the day's trash.

What the hell was he thinking?

Drawing back, Leo raked a hand through his hair, trying to quiet the chaos in his body and brain. But it was hard organizing his thoughts, much less organizing himself.

He hadn't lost it like that in years.

"What's wrong?" Joelle asked tentatively, her face dappled by shadows.

She had a smoky voice, a sexy voice, and yet it seemed so incongruous with her wide aquamarine eyes. She seemed so young still, such a girl, and he felt a rise of protective instinct.

Where the hell were her bodyguards? Where was her grandfather? Her older sisters? Where were those who could help her? Guide her?

Princess Joelle knew far too little about the world. Her family ought to be looking out for her. Instead they'd left her alone in a big city like New Orleans, a city designed to seduce the senses, a city that came alive at night with food and sex and soulful sound.

"What are you doing, *bambina?*" he asked, unable to resist stroking the curve of her cheekbone, her skin irresistibly soft, warm.

He heard the catch in her voice at the gentle caress, but shoulders shifted in a careless shrug. "You know the saying, Leo. Girls just want to have fun."

It was true and not true, Joelle thought as he stared down into her eyes. She wanted a man who craved her. A man who wasn't willing to wait years for her, but had to have her, wanted to be with her as much as she wanted to be with him.

"Fun," he echoed softly and his voice had dropped, deep, low, husky and the word hung there between them so sexual, so seductive that it didn't mean anything remotely fun, but had become a challenge.

He stared down into her eyes for so long she couldn't breathe, the air-choked-off panic spread, sweeping through her, confusing her.

She felt her belly clench, tightening hard, tightening so that she felt strangely empty and the emptiness was painful. She wanted anything but emptiness, anything but pain. "Yes."

She saw him swallow, saw the muscle pull at his jaw. "You'd be better off just going home and cooking up a box of mac and cheese."

Joelle had to bite her tongue. *Mac and cheese.* Macaroni and cheese. Kid stuff. For a kid. Her cheeks burned. She looked away, offended. Affronted. "I'm not a child."

"I didn't say you were."

And suddenly his hand tangled in her long dark hair, his palm wrapping her hair around his fist, once, twice, and with her face forced up, his head descended, his lips again covering hers. The touch of his mouth stunned her, the touch, the pressure so different from before.

She twitched, unnerved, her lips parting in surprise and immediately his lips firmed against her parted mouth, his breath warm, the tip of his tongue just barely brushing the inside of her upper lip.

Joelle jerked, muscles tightening, shuddering and she felt like a papier-mâché puppet on strings. It was the strangest response, nerves, muscles popping, but she couldn't help the hot sharp currents surging through her, or the sudden weakness flooding her limbs, her knees, legs, body dissolving, turning to mush.

Her hands rose, pressed against his chest, struggling to balance herself and somewhere in the back of her brain she thought his chest felt unbelievably hard, smooth, thickly muscled. His body felt the way she'd always imagined a man's body to feel and yet the hand in her hair was no nice-guy touch, but the touch of a possessive man, a sexual man, a man that had no problem marking a woman as his.

This is what she wanted but this isn't what she ought to have. She'd told herself she could have a fling, but Leo Fortino didn't strike her as a nice guy, an easygoing guy, the kind of guy to just let a woman walk away from him.

But you're already promised, her conscience frantically reminded her. You can't break off the engagement.

And I won't, she answered her conscience. This is just one night. One time. Once is all, I promise.

Leo must have felt the indecision, the struggle within her. His head lifted, his lips left hers. She blinked, trying to clear her vision, trying to organize her brain. Say something. Do something. Think smart, funny, fun. But for the life of her nothing came to mind.

Leo broke the silence. "How's that for fun?" he asked, his voice deep, grating against her nerves.

She couldn't answer. Her head and senses swam. She'd felt brave during dinner—so brave she'd been numb—but the numbness was gone and all the fears came rushing back, swamping her.

"Change your mind?" Leo asked softly, and she heard the soft taunt in his voice.

She had, or almost had, knowing that a fling ought to be with someone light, someone easy. Leo was far from light. Deep down Leo—and his sexuality—scared her.

She wanted experience, an affair, but she wanted it on her terms. She wanted a relationship she could control, but if she couldn't control conversation with Leo, how could she hope to control what happened in the bedroom?

''The hotel's around the corner,'' he said, stepping away from her, back onto the pavement, putting distance between them. ''I'll put you in a cab there.''

She followed him out, joining him beneath the street lamp. She felt dazed, dizzy, but certainly not ready to be sent home. ''I'm not running scared.''

Leo's eyes glowed down at her in the dark, the elaborate street lamps of the French Quarter reflecting off his hard features. ''I never said you were.''

''So why put me in a cab?'' She lifted her chin, felt her mouth tremble into a smile. ''I haven't seen the inside of your hotel room yet.''

# CHAPTER FOUR

So SHE was really going to do this.

Leo allowed the door to his hotel suite to swing closed and watched Joelle enter the suite's living room.

The lights were dim. Housekeeping had visited since he left, tidying the suite, turning down the coverlet on his bed, plumping pillows, but Joelle looked calm, nonchalant even as she wandered around the living room.

He couldn't bear to think she did this sort of thing often. He wanted to believe she wasn't promiscuous, or a party girl, but they'd only just met tonight and yet here she was, alone with him in a hotel room at two in the morning.

Yes, he'd invited her here, deliberately tempted her, and it was a test. He was setting her up, testing her values, her morals, and it might not be right, but it was necessary.

He had to know. The wedding was just three weeks away. Three weeks. How could she behave like this just three weeks before their marriage? Did fidelity…loyalty mean nothing? If she tumbled into bed with him, how many other men was she sleeping with? And if she wasn't faithful before the wedding, why should he believe she'd be faithful after?

The acid taste in his mouth burned all the way to his stomach. He'd known women, royal brides, like Joelle who couldn't, wouldn't, be faithful.

He'd known women, prominent beautiful women—models, socialites, princesses—who needed so much emotionally they couldn't be satisfied with just one man, one relationship. He knew how hurtful these women could be. He knew how their insatiable needs wounded those around them, poisoning relationships, scarring their friends and families.

"Something from the bar?" he asked, setting his room key on the table and sliding his jacket off. "Champagne, wine, a cocktail?"

"I'm fine, thank you."

He heard the catch in her voice, heard the nervous edge, and for a moment he felt hope. Relief. Maybe she'd put a stop to this now. He wanted her to put her foot down, be firm, disciplined. He needed her to be a mature woman, one in control of herself, instead of one lost to emotion and whim.

But Joelle turned her back on him, and he saw her examine the suite once again—the subdued elegance of the caramel and bronze interior furnished with pairs of leather club chairs, expensive antiques, and full silk drapes at the window, framing the city nightscape.

"You've a great view of the Mississippi," she said, standing at one of the windows. "I love the river. The action on the river."

He could see the river over her head, spotted the white lights outlining the paddle of a passing steamboat. In the daylight the old paddleboats with their ornate Victorian gingerbread trim looked like miniature wedding cakes.

Wedding cakes. The corner of his mouth curved as cold cynicism ate its way through his heart. Right now there'd be no wedding cake in three weeks. There'd be no wedding at all.

"There's something powerful about water," she added, still studying the river. "I can't imagine not living close to the water, with a view of the water. I think my life has been shaped by tides, storms, boats."

Joelle turned a little, glancing at him over her shoulder. "But you wouldn't have had that where you lived, would you?"

He hesitated a moment, still lost in thought, before forcing himself to answer. "There was the Thames in London, lakes in Switzerland."

Leo shrugged, feeling callous, not wanting to talk about his world anymore. If she wasn't going to be part of his future, she didn't need to know his past.

He crossed to the minibar, opened the small refrigerator and pulled out a bottle of mineral water, popping off the top. He felt as if he were on fire on the inside and he took a long drink, and then another, but the cold mineral water did nothing to cool his temper.

Or his desire.

He wanted her. That was the worst insult of all. He didn't understand how he could feel this kind of anger and betrayal, and yet still be so physically drawn to her.

He shouldn't want her. Shouldn't desire her. She wasn't who she was supposed to be.

It killed him. This wasn't supposed to happen to him. He'd been through this before, had sworn he'd never get trapped by a needy, desperate woman again. And yet here he was, with proof of Joelle's duplicity, and yet unable to act.

He thought he was marrying the innocent Ducasse princess, could remember the discussion with King Remi, Joelle's grandfather, could see the stiff cream folder with gold leaf lying on his desk, the dossier compiled by the Melio palace officials, cross-checked by his own people.

He remembered virtually every word. Every phrase. Every criticism.

*Princess Joelle Ducasse, the youngest of Prince Julien's three daughters, has been overshadowed by her older, more ambitious sisters. Although highly educated, and musically accomplished, Princess Joelle is the least extroverted of the sisters and tends to be retiring, even shy in public.*

He took a long drink, and then another.

*Socially inexperienced, the princess has yet to date, preferring the company of her immediate family over jet-setters her age.*

Leo slammed the bottle on the counter.

Joelle jumped, looked at him wide-eyed. "You're very quiet."

"Just thinking." And he was moving toward her, stalking her, anger, desire, frustration coming together in a vortex of emotion.

He saw a flicker of emotion in her blue-green eyes as he approached her. She was afraid, he thought, and his chest tightened. He didn't want her afraid, but he didn't want her behaving stupidly, either. Life was difficult, demanding, even cruel, and trust was even harder to come by.

He'd grown up without knowing what trust was, grew up needing stability…maturity…normalcy—and it'd been denied. His father had been so eager to get rid of his mother that when the divorce came through, his father had gotten rid of Leo, too, and his father was supposed to be the grounded one. The protective parent.

What a joke.

Leo studied Joelle's pale face, the subtle lift of her chin. He didn't understand her, but he did know this—he couldn't marry a woman who lacked stability, or maturity. He could accept youth—but not immaturity.

Placing his hands on her shoulders, Leo fought his own conflicting emotions, torn between throwing her out and tossing her onto the bed.

He wanted to hold her, touch her, and yet he also knew that there was no future for them. That she was the last woman he could marry. He needed a wife he could depend on, a woman he could trust.

He didn't trust her. He'd never trust her.

It burned within him, the deceit, the deception, and he blamed many for this farce of an engagement, including himself. He should have met Joelle earlier, should have investigated her background more thoroughly.

He'd call her grandfather in the morning. He'd call his own father, the various palace officials. They could break the news to the press any way they wanted. He didn't care how the PR folks handled the broken engagement. Leo just knew he wanted it over, and he wanted it over soon.

Everything felt right and yet wrong, Joelle thought, trapped by the weight of Leo's hands on her shoulders. The attraction between them was tangible. She was hopelessly aware of him, and she knew he desired her, it was there in his eyes, in the touch of his hands, but something else was happening, too...

"Those thoughts seem pretty serious," she whispered as he drew her forward, pulling her toward him.

"Yes."

His one-word answer wasn't half as nerve-wracking as his slow, hot glance. He made her feel like dinner. She swallowed hard, heart racing, her panic growing to the point it crossed her mind that she might have been better off going home.

"How far are you planning on taking this, Josie?" he asked,

hands sliding from her shoulders, down her arms to encircle her wrists.

The moment his fingers circled around hers she felt the hottest current shoot through her hand and up her arm.

The sharp sensation electrified her and every nerve in her screamed for her to run. But her body wouldn't move, her muscles were too weak, too warm.

"How far?" he repeated, drawing her closer still.

Her breath trapped in her throat, bottled in her chest. "Tell me something," she said, awed by the differences between them. He was hard. Very hard. The elegant lines of his suit hid the rugged planes of his chest and the steely-strength of his stomach and thighs.

"What?"

He sounded wary, remote even, his smooth brow furrowed, and yet his intense concentration made him more exotic. A gorgeous sleek animal focused. Deliberating.

She knew he must have his pick of women. He was gorgeous, sophisticated, intelligent, wealthy…sexual. She swallowed the butterflies back, her body alive with nervous energy. "You said earlier you wanted my body, and my mind."

He stared at her, said nothing, just waiting.

Her mouth was drying out. She had to swallow again but she couldn't come up with any moisture. "And I was wondering…and forgive me for being blunt, but why would you find me interesting? I'm twenty-two. You're ten years older. What would I have, intellectually, that would appeal to you?"

He didn't answer, but his mouth compressed, his lovely mouth with firm, mobile lips, tightened, and as his silence lengthened, she knew.

He wanted her mind because it was attached to her body, but it wasn't her mind he wanted. It was her body.

"I haven't answered yet, so don't go putting words in my mouth," he said, tipping her chin up. "And yes, your body is beautiful but you've talent—don't forget, I heard you sing tonight—you also play guitar and you probably play other instruments as well."

"The piano and violin," she said, swallowing the lump in her throat.

"You're educated, apparently well-traveled, fluent in three languages—"

"Four."

One eyebrow arched. "What's the fourth?"

"Spanish."

"Of course." The corner of his mouth tugged. "And even though you were dressed like a Vegas showgirl earlier, you've beautiful manners."

"And men like nice manners?"

He grimaced wryly. "Some of us do." His teasing smile faded. "But what's happening here isn't about love, it's sex. But I think you know that. And I think it's sex you want."

The word sex sounded so bald, so blunt, and it bounced around her head like a Ping-Pong ball. Sex. Sex with Leo. Sex because she wanted to know more, wanted to have an experience that was hers, and hers alone...sex because it was her choice, her own choice, and probably the last thing that would ever be her choice.

"If you're hoping for more," he added, "you're not—"

"I understand," she cut him off.

His lashes had dropped, his expression concealed. "You don't have to stay."

"I understand that, too." She felt as if he was trying to get rid of her, trying to send her packing and she didn't understand it. He wanted her, but he didn't want her. He was attracted but he fought the attraction. She sensed that beneath all the hardness and cool sophistication, he was very true, maybe even old-fashioned.

It was a shame she wasn't someone else. It was a shame they'd met this way.

For a moment Joelle was filled with indecision, the unknown yawning about her in every direction, and then she did what she knew she needed to do. She touched him. She placed her hands tentatively on his chest, needing to discover him, needing to discover herself, life and sex.

Yet touching him wasn't without pain. With her hands on his

chest, his dress shirt the only thing between her skin and his, she wondered if this was how she was supposed to feel. Conflicted. Wrenched. Overwhelmed.

Touching him made her feel, and her heart felt so tender right now, all her emotions stirred.

His hands moved to her back, and he drew her even closer. "Cold?" he asked, as she shuddered at his touch.

"No." She felt the heat of his body as well as the power of his thighs and hips. He felt hard, aroused, and the ridge in his trousers pushed against her flat belly. "Adrenaline."

"Adrenaline?"

"I think the suspense is killing me." She was scared and yet turned on. Anxious. Excited. "I'm—" She broke off, knowing she couldn't just tell him she was relatively inexperienced, knowing that men were put off by confessions of innocence. She didn't want to risk putting him off. If she only had this one night with him she wanted it to be perfect. "Never mind. It's nothing."

His head dropped, his face close to hers, capturing the warmth of her skin, the flutter of her breath, before his lips touched hers, slowly. It was a light caress and yet there was something fierce behind it, something so hot, so dangerous that she turned her head away, afraid of the flare of heat.

His hand slid up her back, beneath her hair to cup her nape. She tingled every place his hand had touched.

"Your heart's racing," he said as she buried her face against his shirt, drinking in the smell of him, so sensitive to his warmth, his strength, the very texture of his skin.

"You have that effect on me."

He tipped her head back, stared into her eyes. "I bet you say that to all the men."

"No." She tried to smile but failed. Instead she reached up, touched his face. He jerked at her light touch but didn't pull away.

Slowly she trailed her fingertips from his chin—flat across the bottom with just a hint of a cleft—to the strong sweep of jaw. She wanted to know the shape of his face, the lines in his cheekbone and chin, the fragrance that was part skin, part sultry New Orleans tropics. It was like moonlight, musk and jasmine.

"You have a beautiful face," she whispered, awed by the bristles of his beard, the firmness of his skin.

"I don't. It's ordinary."

"There's nothing ordinary about you." She felt him smile and drawing back a little she saw that the corner of his mouth had indeed curved in what she'd come to recognize as his mocking smile. She'd never met any man so young and old. How could he be so jaded at thirty-two?

His smile faded as his eyes met hers, and his dark head dipped, his mouth covering hers again. Oh, how she liked the feel of his mouth against her, liked the smell of him and pressure.

Teasing, she thought, eyes closing, he was teasing her with that warm fleeting touch. It was the perfect seductive kiss—like breathing the aroma of a fine red wine before actually sipping—wakening the senses, stirring the imagination. The tantalizing pressure of his lips seemed to say a kiss wasn't just a kiss, it was pleasure itself.

Then he deepened the kiss, one hand rising to cup her cheek, his thumb stroking near her mouth and hot sensation flooded her limbs, sending rivulets of feeling everywhere. She was melting on the inside even as her breasts ached, her nipples peaking, incredibly sensitive.

Her response stirred him, and heat flared, hot, raw and the kiss changed. No longer tentative, or teasing, Leo's lips were firm, demanding, taking, tasting.

He teased the upper bow of her lip with his tongue and when her lips parted beneath his, he traced the shape of her mouth, the delicate skin inside her lower lip, and then her cheek, the tip of her tongue, saying without words that he would have her and enjoy her but it'd be strictly on his terms.

His hand slid from her cheek, down her neck, over her collarbone to cup her breast. Joelle shuddered at the brush of his fingertips over her nipple. He caressed her again and her belly clenched, tight, hot, aching.

He made her want so much, and the desire made her confident.

This was right, she thought, this was how a first time should be. Powerful. Sensual. Sexual. And his hand slipped beneath her blouse, his palm warm on her bare abdomen, fingers light against her narrow rib cage.

She dragged in another breath, trying to clear her head, trying to shake some of the dizziness away but his touch was too warm, too pleasurable.

When he lifted the edge of the silk of her bra cup, his warm skin against her warmer breast Joelle took a strangled breath and thought for sure she'd melt, dissolving into pure endless need.

No one had ever touched her like this…

No one had ever made her so helpless and hungry at the same time.

She could imagine his hands on her belly, on her hips, between her thighs. It might hurt, she thought, heart pounding, but then it might not, and even if it did hurt, how much better that it happen this way. With him. With someone as sensual and knowledgeable as Leo Fortino.

Suddenly Leo was pushing her backward, setting her firmly down on the edge of the bed.

Dizzily she braced herself, her head spinning, her hands braced on either side of her hips.

Leo stood above her, tall, silent, considering, the electricity between them tangible. She saw the dark flush in his cheekbones, the storm of passion in his green eyes. He was breathing deep, his chest filling, rising, and his lips pressed hard.

Abruptly he leaned forward, wrapped his hand in her hair, lifted her face to his and kissed her hard, a searing kiss, open mouth, a kiss of tongues, a kiss where he took her breath and total possession of her. It was as if he was opening her, rendering her vulnerable, rendering her his.

And as his tongue swept her mouth, probed her mouth, making her want to hold his tongue in her mouth, capturing the fierce rhythmic thrusts that made her belly clench and clench again. The kiss made her think of his hard body on hers, in hers, and heat flooded her womb, sent blood to all the places already far too sensitive.

Fingers still tangled in her hair, he turned his head, ending the kiss. "Take your clothes off," he commanded hoarsely, the bristles of his beard rough against her jaw, his warm breath tickling her skin.

The command, so hard, so direct sent flickers of feeling everywhere. Joelle shivered and clutched at the silk coverlet on the bed.

There were moments she forgot about his power, his authority, but all it took was one demand for her to realize he'd always been in control. That he'd never lose, much less give up, control to her. "Now?" she choked.

He'd straightened and he stood over her, warrior-like, and his dark green gaze stripped her naked. "Yes."

She wanted this, she reminded herself, she wanted to know life.

Wanted to know about power and possession.

Heart thudding, she reached for the strings of her blouse where it was tied in the small of her back. She felt his gaze, felt his intense concentration. Her hands shook as she fiddled with the knot, struggling to undo it.

Seconds crawled. Time slowed. His gaze grew harder. Hotter.

Hands damp, she finally got the knot undone and ties loosened she reached for the hem of her blouse and drew it up over her head and set it on the bed next to her.

He said nothing.

He did nothing.

Joelle blushed, feeling foolish in her faded jeans and push-up bra.

The jeans, she told herself. And standing, nearly bumping into Leo, she unfastened the snap, undid the zipper and breathing shallowly, air hard to come by, she pushed the jeans down over her hips, down her legs until she stepped out of those.

The jeans joined the blouse on the foot of the bed.

She was wearing very simple white silk underwear—white silk panties, the white silk push-up bra. And in her white undergarments she felt even more naked than before.

She glanced up at Leo, saw nothing encouraging in his face, and tears pricked the back of her eyes. Why was she doing this? What was she doing here?

And yet she knew. She was giving her virginity to Leo Fortino to keep from giving it to Luigi Borgarde, Prince of Milano, Count of Venetio, or whatever his official title was.

Although she did think it rather telling that she didn't even know his proper title.

But I'm not marrying for love, she flashed back, tearful, miserable. I've never even met Luigi before. He didn't even try to meet me before the engagement was announced. Instead he just sent some official to the palace, some Borgarde representative to look me up and down, and have me sign the necessary paperwork.

Paperwork. I'm a contract bride. A bargain basement princess. A blue-light special.

Scalding tears burned the back of her eyes and she knew why she never let herself think about Luigi Borgarde. She didn't let herself think about him because she was furious with him, furious that he actually thought it was okay to enter her world, move into her palace, take her parents' old bedroom without ever asking her to her face if she'd like to marry him.

How could a man, a real man, send a representative to handle the engagement?

How could a real man think a woman wanted to be treated like a business deal?

Was it really too much for Prince Luigi to take a day out of his business schedule to meet his future wife? She'd asked Grandpapa to arrange a meeting, asked more than once to allow them time to get to know each other before the engagement was announced to the public, but Grandpapa had said the prince was busy, and that she ought to trust him. *He's a good man,* her grandfather replied, *he's exactly what you, and Melio, need.*

The anger burned hotter, the anger nearly drowning out her passion.

Her grandfather might know what Melio needed, but he didn't know what *she* needed. He didn't know what *she* wanted. No one but Grandmama ever knew her, everyone else assuming she was like Nic and Chantal, assuming duty meant everything.

But duty was the last thing she cared about. Instead she loved music. Passionately, fiercely, with all her heart. When she sang, when she played her guitar, she wasn't a poor princess, or a princess without any position or power. She felt strong. Capable. Beautiful.

The tears continued to burn and gather. Her throat felt raw and the pain she never let herself dwell on threatened to suffocate her. If the Ducasses had been wealthier, if Melio had stronger financial resources—like oil, or exports—she could have married whomever she wished.

Instead she was marrying a stranger because he was wealthy and she was not. Her prince wanted children and she needed heirs. He wanted her kingdom and she—a woman—couldn't rule Melio without a man.

"If you've changed your mind...?" Leo's voice sounded above her head, bringing her back from the life that waited for her in Europe. The life she'd return to tomorrow.

Joelle shook her head, once, twice, fiercely. So many important choices taken from her, so much decided, determined, for her. She'd had this one night. She'd be with Leo, make love because she wanted to make love, to feel something special because it was what she wanted. It was what she *needed*.

"Nothing's changed," she answered, and yet her voice broke.

Pulse racing, Joelle reached behind her back and struggled to unhook her silk bra, peeling the delicate fabric from her shoulders and breasts.

Her hands shook and yet defiantly she lifted her chin, looked up into Leo's eyes. I want to do this, she silently repeated, I want to make love because it's the one thing I can choose for myself, the one thing no one can take from me, the one thing that will mean something to me even when I return home.

Eyes dark, expression shuttered, Leo joined her on the bed. She held her breath as he moved forward, straddling her legs, his knees outside her own. He wasn't even touching her yet, but she felt the warmth of him anyway.

This was it, she thought, the real thing.

And with him so big, so dark above her, she suddenly doubted her ability to see this through.

What did she really know about making love? What did she know about men's bodies?

She closed her eyes as his hands settled on her thighs, the pressure from his hands firm. Compelling. She wasn't going anywhere.

"So," he said, hands sliding ever so slowly up the length of her thighs sending rivers of feeling everywhere. "I take it you're protected?"

Protected? She felt a wall of heat slam through her. She'd forgotten all about that aspect. "Oh, right. Yes." She struggled to sit up but he was above her, still dressed, his body so large, so powerful. "I have um, a—" she looked up, saw the lift of his eyebrows "—a…condom…in my purse."

"You carry your own?"

No, actually, at least, she hadn't until tonight. But tonight she'd grabbed one from the dispenser in the women's bathroom at the club tonight. Just in case.

"I thought I…um, should," she stumbled, but he said nothing, let her flail about, waiting for more. It amazed her how he did that. He got so much information from her by just sitting back, waiting, letting her fill the awkward silences. "You know, take precautions."

"As you should," he answered, leaning forward to grab a leather satchel from the night table. He opened the leather bag, a men's shaving kit with all the gear one would expect before locating a foil pouch. "But I do have my own."

He set the foil pouch on the bed, next to her shoulder, and leaning over he kissed her shoulder. Her nipples peaked, breasts aching. She felt so bare and yet he was in no hurry to touch her.

She drew another quick breath when his lips found the crazy pulse in the small hollow below her ear. She was melting into a molten pool of need.

His lips trailed down her neck, slowly, very slowly until his mouth rested on her collarbone. "Undress me," he said.

His voice vibrated against her skin, sending shock waves through her, shock waves nearly as strong as her jittery response.

"Undress you?" He was so close, so very much on top of her and yet to reach the buttons on his shirt she had to sit higher, leaning toward him.

"Yes."

Joelle felt so exposed, her breasts bare, her hair loose, naked except for her miniscule panties. But she forced herself to ignore her nudity, forced herself to think only of him.

Leaning closer, she breathed in scent of his cologne, the deep woodsy spice, concentrated on the seductive heat of his body. Ignoring the trembling of her hands, she focused her line of sight on the very first button on his shirt. Determined, she undid the button and then moved to the next.

Before she knew it they were both naked and she was lying beneath him. She felt a little foolish, and very inexperienced as he reached out and stroked his hand down her body, from her breast to her hip. Joelle shivered, nipples peaking.

"Nothing's happened yet," he said, stretching out next to her.

"Am I that unappealing?"

He made a sound, half laugh, half growl. "You're very appealing."

# CHAPTER FIVE

HE DIPPED his head, kissed her, taking his time, slowing the kiss down, slowing Joelle's frantic pulse until she could think of nothing but him and his skin and her desire to be closer to him.

She wanted to feel him on her. In her. She wanted to feel his heat and strength properly.

His hands cupped her breasts, palms grazing across her taut nipples and then down to shape her ribs, her waist, her hips.

He had a great sense of touch, a way of making her feel soft and hot in all the right places. And when his mouth touched the hollow of her neck she gasped, reached for him, let her arms curl around his shoulders. She loved the feel of his body, the hard smooth tension beneath his skin and her fingers gripped the thick muscles of his upper arms as his mouth alternately kissed and bit across her own shoulder and collarbone. She hadn't imagined she could feel anything there, but his teeth and tongue found hundreds of nerve endings that were begging to be stroked and licked and nipped.

With his hands moving across her thighs, between her thighs, and his mouth drawing trails of fire across her breast she felt wild with need.

Helplessly she arched up against him, pressing herself closer, wanting more, wanting the terrible ache inside of her answered.

She sighed as his lips closed around one swollen nipple, sighed again as he parted her thighs with his knee, making room for him. The air felt cool against her skin, she felt so open as he shifted his weight, one leg and then another moving between her knees.

She shuddered as he lifted his head, looked down on her, looked to see her spread out before him. Joelle felt strangely like a sacrificial offering and it crossed her mind—fleetingly—that this is how it would have been on her wedding night if she'd waited, except she wouldn't have been half so attracted, half so turned on. Much better her first time be now, with Leo. Much better she do this her way, have something like this be her choice, within her control.

"I'm losing you," he said, his voice so husky it rasped across her senses, stirring her all over again.

"No. I'm here."

"You're deep in thought."

She reached up to touch his face, marveling at the feel of his beard-roughened jaw. "Just thinking about you."

His black eyebrow arched. He didn't believe it. She smiled. "Do you have so little faith in me?"

His expression hardened, dark green eyes burning hot and fierce. "I don't trust easily."

"Good. Neither do I." And she brought his face down to hers, kissed him slowly, kissed him the same way he'd kissed her earlier, and as the kiss deepened she felt his resistance dissolve.

He shifted, leaned up over her, his hips lowering against her pelvis.

The insistent press of his erection took her breath away, the rigid length between them, hard and hot against her tummy.

"I want you," she said, gathering her courage.

"I'm here."

"Not inside me yet."

And then suddenly he was there, hard against her tender skin, his big body pushing forward. She was warm, slick, but he didn't enter her easily, her body tensing.

Joelle felt his hand move between them, touch her, touch her readiness before he took his shaft in his hand, rubbed the tip across her delicate folds, stroking her once, twice, and she responded instinctively, opening her legs wider, hands moving to Leo's hips.

He stroked his shaft across her once more and as she lifted her hips for him she felt him slide into her, an inch or two and her mouth opened in surprise, stunned by the stretch, the sting of pain.

He pressed harder and again she felt him pull and stretch her. Was this how it felt for everyone? Did it always hurt like this?

Fighting panic, Joelle took a breath, exhaled, tried to relax. And as she said told herself to relax, this was normal, he was just breaking through the hymen, she felt him thrust forward, hard. Harder than she expected. Hard enough her eyes smarted, tears suddenly welling.

She must have made a sound because he stopped moving, lifted his head to look down at her. "Did I hurt you?"

She was panting a little on the inside, trying to get adjusted to his size, trying to accept the feel of him. "You're big."

"Should I stop?"

"No." She pressed her hands to the hollow of his back, her fingers clenched into small, frightened fists. It actually hurt more than she'd expected, and maybe she should have said something to Leo, let him know she didn't have the experience, that she'd never...

Too late anyway, she told herself, trying not to feel so alone, so scared. This was what she wanted to do, this is how she'd wanted it to happen.

"I won't move until it stops hurting," he said, his head dipping to kiss her gently. "Your body just needs to get used to mine."

He sounded very wise and she was grateful for this bit of advice, especially as he was still kissing her, less gently, more passionately, his lips teasing hers, his tongue stroking her tongue, his mouth taking her mind off what was happening in the rest of her body.

This was a kiss, she thought, head spinning, body rippling with delicious sensations and then she shifted beneath Leo and found that the painful sensation had lessened and instead she just felt oddly full, flushed, sensitive.

He started to move, small thrusts of his hips and she felt a ripple of sensation unlike the other sensations, this one a whisper of excitement, a flutter of delicious pleasure. She took a breath, shifted, lifting her hips to see if she could feel it again and he thrust harder, deeper and the pleasure returned, stronger, brighter, like strokes of cobalt-blue against white, color exploding in her mind's eye. And Leo took the lead, thrusting deeply, withdrawing to thrust again and the pleasure of it dazzled her.

He touched her body in so many places and so many ways but it wasn't what she thought sex would feel like. It was a thousand times better.

Her pulse had quickened, her skin felt hot, and as he drove into her she began to tighten on the inside, trying to grip him, hold him, keep him with her but he wouldn't let her hold him, wouldn't let her stop him and the friction built, hot, hotter until her muscles were tightening, tensing on their own, a fierce white-hot heat growing, threatening to explode.

"I can't—"

"Let it go," he answered in her ear, and she shook her head not certain what to do, or how to do it.

"Let it go," he repeated, his hips rocking deep, rocking her keeping her from escaping the delicious torment and just when she didn't think she could hold on, hold back, her body went— a stinging flicker bursting into flame. She shuddered helplessly beneath him, her body gripping his tightly, so tightly, her muscles rippling to life.

She felt his hands bury in her hair, felt his lips brush hers and he groaned her name before arching, tensing, and she felt him go, just as she had.

Later, she wasn't sure when, but she stirred, realized he was still with her, in her, and she felt his gaze, felt him watching her. "What are you doing?" she asked, stretching a little.

"Looking at you."

"Why?"

"You're beautiful."

She smiled shyly and he dropped a kiss on her lips before pulling away. He left the bed momentarily, headed for the bathroom and Joelle reached for the bedcovers and then realized when Leo reappeared from the bathroom that he'd merely discarded the condom.

How silly of her to worry. But how personal it all was. How intimate.

She flushed, embarrassed as she saw him approach the bed, big, muscular, naked. But her embarrassment faded as he climbed into bed, slid between the covers and pulled her back into his arms.

His skin was still warm, a little damp and she nestled closer, feeling incredibly safe. It was so hard to believe they'd just...and it felt like...

"Amazing," she murmured.

"You think?"

She laughed softly, stunned, happy, happy stunned. "Tonight has been..." Her voice drifted off. There were no words. Even if she wanted to explain it to him, share some of the significance of the night, he'd never really know what this—them—meant to her.

With a sigh, Joelle rolled over onto her back, stared up at the ceiling. Her heart was still beating fast. Her skin felt deliciously warm and damp. "I know I'm repeating myself, but I wish I had more time here. I'm not ready to go. There's so much I still want to do. I'd love to play tourist."

"That's the reason you don't want to go home?"

"No. I don't want to go home because I don't want to go to work, but the reason I don't want to leave here is that I love New Orleans." She turned, looked at him, nose wrinkling. "That didn't make any sense, did it?"

"Limited sense."

She laughed a little, savored Leo's gorgeousness. His name suited him. He looked so virile, so primal in bed. All golden muscles. All sexual power. "I've been here nearly a year and there's so much I haven't done yet."

"Such as?"

He reached out, brushed her hair from her breast, letting his palm cover her instead.

She shivered with pleasure as his warm palm cupped her, rubbing lightly, maddeningly across her nipple.

"All of it."

Eyes closed, Joelle pictured the Louisiana she'd yet to see, the colorful brochures pushed on tourists from endless city kiosks. "I'd love to have done the plantation tours, swamp tours, ghost tours, French Quarter walking tours—"

"You're joking." He gently pinched her nipple.

She squirmed against his hand, her body rippling to life all over again, her insides warming, her thighs feeling liquid and hot.

"No." She could hardly speak. She knew now how his body felt on hers, in hers, and she wanted it again. The pleasure. The pressure. The full sensation. But she couldn't be wanton, couldn't demand more, couldn't ask for another go at it. There ought to be some self-control.

She forced herself to think about her tourist wish list instead.

"I'd love a trip to Audobon Park and the zoo," she inhaled, his hand so warm against her breast, the heat intense, making her ache. "A ride on the streetcar, a Mississippi Riverboat cruise, the usual."

"Look at me."

His voice crackled authority, control, and she could only do as he asked. Her lashes lifted and she stared into his eyes, his eyes so dark they looked almost black, like the forest at night, like pine trees with just a hint of moonlight and her heart squeezed.

"You've been here a year, *bella*. Haven't you done any of that?"

She was lost, she thought, lost in him, and she'd done the unthinkable by going to bed with him. She'd given him not just her body, but her heart.

Stupid Jo. Stupid stupid Jo.

"I've been working." She tried to smile, tried to hide the intense emotions filling her. "If it's not one job, it's another."

"Maybe tomorrow," he said.

"Maybe," she answered, knowing tomorrow would be too late.

He didn't say anything and she felt his ambivalence, sympathy maybe. "Don't look at me like that," she said, pulling away from him, pushed on her elbow. "I may look young, but I know everyone has to grow up sometime. Even rebels like me."

He lifted a strand of her hair, twined it around his finger. "I don't worry. I'm the action type. I do what needs to be done."

"Like tonight?" she teased, trying to hide the depth of her emotion. She felt funny on the inside. Tender. Bruised. The sex had been so good, the time with him unreal and yet she knew she was supposed to get up and leave. Walk away. Never look back.

He tugged on the strand of her hair, a sharp painful tug that drew smart tears to her eyes. "This is just the beginning, *bella*."

But it wasn't the beginning, she thought, trying to blink away the tears. It was the end...the end, at least, of what they had here. "So how was I? Good? Bad? Average?" she asked, trying to figure out if he had any idea that she'd been so inexperienced.

"You're asking for a performance assessment?"

She wanted to laugh but couldn't. You didn't just lose your virginity every day. "Yes."

His dark gaze roamed her face. He loosened the tendril of hair wrapped around his finger and smoothed her hair back from her face. "You were good. Very good."

She didn't know why she felt such a strong need to please him. Maybe it was because she wanted him to enjoy the lovemaking as much as she did. It only seemed right that he felt half the pleasure she'd felt. "You're certain I didn't do anything stupid?"

He rubbed at the worry lines between her brows. "You shouldn't ever worry about such a thing—"

"Women do."

He sighed, shook his head. "Well, you shouldn't. You're gorgeous. You felt unbelievable."

"Good," she answered softly, trying to smile but sadness replaced her anxiety. How odd...this...how bittersweet.

Her first time with Leo.

Her last time with Leo.

Joelle moved closer to him, curving her body against his, not ready to go, not certain she'd ever be really ready. No one had ever held her so close, and yet she knew she'd have to leave soon. Put her clothes on. Head home.

"Stay the night," he said, lightly tracing her spine, his fingertips following the vertebrae until he reached the hollow, the indentation filled with sensitive nerve endings.

"Most men don't like that sort of thing."

"What sort of thing?"

"You know. A woman sleeping over. Commitment."

He laughed. "You know too much about the world, *bambina*. You're only twenty-two."

"I do have older sisters."

"You're close to them?"

"Used to be."

"What happened?"

Her shoulders shifted. "We all grew up."

Leo stirred, and his expression suddenly looked distant. Remote. "I have a conference call scheduled for the morning, but you don't have to leave. I can make the call from the next room."

"Important call?"

Very important, he thought. He'd be calling her grandfather, calling his own father. It wouldn't be a pleasant call.

It wouldn't be a pleasant day at all.

Suddenly Joelle kissed his chest, a little above his nipple, her lips soft and warm against his skin. "Then go to sleep. You'll need your sleep. The last thing you need to do is worry about me."

Joelle woke. It was early, not yet five-thirty in the morning. She dressed quietly in the bathroom, careful not to wake Leo.

She was terrible with goodbyes, had never liked them, but saying goodbye to Leo seemed worse than uncomfortable—it'd be impossible.

After a night in Leo's arms, she felt emotionally spent. She'd known he'd be a one-time only, and while part of her mind was trying to accept it, another part—the part that had yielded to him completely—couldn't let go.

*You knew though, there'd be just one night,* she lectured herself, hooking her bra. *You knew it was a once-in-a-lifetime fling.* For one night she'd been someone she wasn't supposed to be. She'd been free, warm, passionate. She'd blown caution to the wind, she'd experienced what most women her age were allowed to experience. And that was the beauty of it. For one night she'd been just Joelle and not a princess, and not public property, and not under a microscope.

She'd loved that everything between her and Leo was private. No one would know. No one *needed* to know.

Dressed—except the panties that had gone missing—Joelle dragged her fingers through her hair, pulling the long strands into a loose ponytail. She had a hair elastic in her pocket and she fastened the ponytail at her nape. It was messy, but it worked.

Leaving the bathroom she grabbed her shoes, headed to the living room where she sat down at the elegant writing desk. Using the hotel's pad of paper and pen she tried to scribble Leo a note, but after writing his name, she didn't know what to say.

She stared blankly at the paper. Swallowed. Knew there wasn't much time. *Say something.*

Again she put the pen to paper, hesitated briefly and then just began writing. Soon she'd filled the page. She hoped the words, and thanks, would make sense.

Joelle returned to the bedroom, placed the note on Leo's side of the bed. He was asleep, one muscular arm above his head, his face turned into the crook of his arm. She watched him for a moment, trying to take it all in, wanting to remember the details, the size of him, the shape, the way he seemed to fill not just the bed, but the very room.

She knew she'd never see him again. And yet she also knew he wasn't a man she'd ever forget.

Her veneer of control slipped the moment she walked through the hotel's pretty lobby and exited through the glass front doors.

The sky was still dark except for a slice of steely gray on the horizon and drawing a deep breath, Joelle drew the cool air, heavy with moisture, into her lungs.

She'd thought a night with Leo would answer all her questions, would quell that burning need to know what sex was all about, and yes, the questions had been answered all right. She didn't just like sex. She liked Leo. A lot.

The bell captain assisted her into the back of a waiting taxi and as the cab pulled away from the hotel entrance, Joelle slouched down low on the seat, insides hot, tight, churning.

*Don't think about it. Don't think about him. Just don't go there.*

Staring blindly out the window, she saw the moment the sun broke through the layers of cloud, turning the sky the faintest shade of pinky gray. And that dusty pink reminded her of Brennan's and the carriage entrance on Royal Street and the feel of Leo's mouth taking hers.

*Stop thinking.*

Joelle closed her eyes, pressed her thumb to her mouth. Too late for regrets, she told herself. There's nothing you can do about anything now. What's been done has been done. But that didn't help the ache inside her heart.

She'd been prepared for the worst-case scenario. Not the best case. She'd wanted to know what it was like to make love with a real man. To be held in the arms of a man with strength and power, as well as expertise and control.

Well, she'd found out.

Exhaling a little, she pressed her thumb harder against her bottom lip, feeling the softness and soreness, the soreness a memory of a night spent kissing. Making love.

And oh, they'd made love. He'd initiated her into aspects of lovemaking she hadn't known existed, found pleasure in endless varieties of touch. He'd stirred her, tormented her, pleasured her.

Another quick inhale, and Joelle opened her eyes, feeling her chest tighten and burn.

He'd felt so right against her. His skin had felt smooth, sleek, sensuous, warm.

Never had she read anything about the bliss of skin.

Never had anyone spoken to her about the calm even in the eye of the storm.

Never had she suspected such fire, such fierceness, such beauty...and it had been beautiful. It had felt better than anything she'd ever imagined, felt wild, felt strong, felt like a primitive woman. Hungry. Alive. Demanding.

She'd wanted everything from him. She'd wanted to give everything back.

And she knew it wasn't going to be like this with Prince Borgarde. Not even on their best day. And she knew—too late—that no knowledge might actually have been a better thing than some knowledge.

"What's the address again?" the driver asked, breaking the silence.

Joelle saw that they'd reached her neighborhood. "The next block. The brick building on the left side, the one with the black shutters."

Climbing the stairs to her second-floor apartment, Joelle felt the tightness return to her chest, but there wasn't time to do anything but climb into the shower and face the day.

The shower spray pelted warm and hard but it was little relief. She couldn't stop thinking about him. Or the way she felt in his arms. Or the way he'd stretched her out beneath him, his hands on her wrists as he extended her arms high over her head and each time his body dipped into hers she rose with her hips to meet him.

It had been so instinctive. So good. She'd relished the sensation, the pressure, the slow slide of his skin across hers.

The heat of his body…

The strength of his thigh…

The way he kissed her neck just below her jaw…

Reluctantly she turned off the water and stood in the shower, head pressed to the wet tiles, the water dripping off of her.

How had it gone so wrong? Where had she made the mistake? It was going to be easy. She'd thought the whole thing out—analyzed the situation, considered the different scenarios, the various angles it could all play out—and she'd been prepared to suffer a little bruised feelings…a little defeat.

But it hadn't ever crossed her mind that she'd fall for him seriously. She'd thought that good sex or bad sex, she'd at least have experience, but what was happening inside of her had nothing to do with sex at all.

A knock sounded on the outside of the bathroom door. It was Lacey, Joelle's roommate. "Josie, you better hurry. You don't want to miss your flight."

Joelle grabbed a towel. "I'm on my way."

Leo knew Joelle was gone the moment he woke up. He knew before he'd even opened his eyes, and for a few seconds he lay there, arm covering his eyes, seething with frustration.

He wasn't supposed to have slept with her.

He was supposed to have stopped things before they got out of hand.

How the hell had he lost such complete control? He *never* lost control. He was the master of cool, the perfect gentleman as one ex-lover had complained.

Yet he had lost control, and it had been the wrong time, wrong woman, wrong situation altogether.

Livid with himself, Leo threw back the duvet, swung his legs out, and spotting a scrap of white silk—Joelle's panties—between the bisque sheets, he reached down to retrieve them. He froze.

Leo looked up, toward the bedroom door, which stood partway open, and then back down at the bottom sheet. The faint red stain suddenly looked much darker, but that was his imagination. She wasn't a virgin. She couldn't be.

There was no way she was still a virgin, and even if she were, why would she lose her virginity just weeks before her wedding? It didn't make sense. None of it made sense. But his gut felt like he'd swallowed a lead weight.

He'd outlawed the practice of taking virgins years ago, deciding that virgins were for younger men. More sensitive men. Men that still had youth and patience on their side. He had neither. Closing in on thirty-five he'd had women, many women, and he knew what he wanted and what he didn't want.

He'd wanted to prove that Joelle was a fraud...a phony...not the perfect princess the Melio palace had tried to convince him he was getting. So he'd set out to prove them wrong. And he'd seduced her, deliberately seduced her, knowing perfectly well that he was using his expertise with his hands, his body, using his knowledge of a woman's body to bring her to her knees, and yet all the while he'd assumed...

Was so sure...

Exhaling, Leo shook his head, even as little bits of last night returned to him, impressions that had come and gone.

Like her uncertainty at different points, and her body, tight, narrow, tense. It'd been difficult entering her, but he'd put it down to nerves, and yet...

Leo sighed, rubbed his forehead, forced himself to go back, remember.

There'd been resistance, almost a barrier, and he'd wondered briefly, very briefly, if she'd never made love before but she'd said nothing, she'd just reached for him, encouraged him and he—passion blind—had gone.

Had pushed through, pushed into her.

God. The heaviness in his gut seeped through the rest of his body.

Sick on the inside, he climbed from bed and spotted the hotel notepad on the nightstand. A note from Joelle. Cursing, he picked up the notepad, read what she'd written. *Maldezione,* he cursed again.

*Leo, I couldn't have asked for a better "first" time, or a more generous lover. Thank you for everything. You were wonderful. Fondly, Josie.*

He went cold. Ice cold. His throat worked as he struggled to swallow his shock.

It was a thank-you letter.

She'd left him a thank-you letter. *For taking her virginity.*

Hell.

*Hell.*

What was she thinking? What was she doing?

The whole thing was too ludicrous for words. He'd never been thanked before for doing this, much less in such a polite manner with the overriding theme being thank you but we're finished. He'd taken her virginity and now she was giving him what amounted to a very polite brush-off.

The ice melted, giving way to poker-hot rage. Dropping the pad on the night table, Leo reached for the phone, then realized he didn't have her home phone number.

Cursing yet again, he slammed the phone back into the cradle, sat down on the edge of the bed, read the note once more.

*I couldn't have asked for a better "first" time, or a more generous lover.*

*Couldn't have asked...*

The words went round and round in his brain and his temper grew, threatening to explode. What was she doing? Thinking?

How could she allow herself to be seduced three weeks before her wedding?

It didn't make sense.

*She* didn't make sense.

He'd thought he'd had her all figured out. Thought she was fast, loose, wanton. She'd been good in bed, but he'd thought it was experience that made her so responsive, not…what? Curiosity? Eagerness? Passion?

The questions screamed at him. Why him, and why last night? Why the seduction three weeks before the wedding? Was she trying to get out of the marriage? And if she wasn't, how could she let a stranger—which is what she thought he was—take what was rightfully her fiancé's?

Rising from the bed, Leo stalked naked to the bathroom. He was angry. Very angry. Last night had been good, and she'd been better than good. She'd been liquid fire in his bed, so hot, so fierce, so everything he'd wanted in a woman, so everything he was sure he'd never find.

But to find it in Joelle, his fiancée, a woman he doubted at every level? How was it possible?

The questions ate at him as he showered, continued to eat him as he shaved and brushed his teeth. He needed answers now. No more games. No more hiding. He only wanted the truth.

Leo felt a savage emotion fill him as he exited the hotel. His driver was waiting outside in the circular brick driveway, the black Mercedes gleaming between lush tropical palm fronds.

"The French Quarter," Leo said grimly, climbing in the back seat, giving Joelle's home address.

Traffic was light on Canal Street and they reached her neighborhood in minutes. Leo didn't even wait for the driver to open the door for him. Instead he leapt from the back of the Mercedes sedan.

Leaving him a note. A *note*. A *thank-you* note.

He flashed to the night before, recalled her sweetness in bed, her skin so soft, her taste like honey. She'd felt even better than she'd looked, and when she'd melted into him, against him, her body curved to meet his in all the right ways. She was more erotic than any woman he'd ever known and she was a virgin.

And not just any virgin. His virgin, and what had to be the last of the virgin princesses. And the fact that his princess, his virgin, would give it up to a stranger made him madder than hell.

Leo's gut hurt as he rang her doorbell. So she'd wanted experience? She'd wanted a good "first time"? Great. He'd show her prowess in bed. He'd show her a lot more than he did last night. He'd teach the little minx everything she'd ever want to know.

And he'd enjoy every goddamn minute of it, too.

He rang the doorbell again. And finally minutes later, the door opened and a young woman peered out, curly hair disheveled, a white bathrobe wrapped about her slender frame. "Can I help you?" she asked, hands encircling a ceramic coffee mug.

He glanced up at the house number above the painted door. "I'm looking for Josie d'Ville."

"She's gone."

"To work? The store? Where?" he demanded roughly, unable to hide his impatience. He had so many questions he had to ask her. So much he needed to understand.

The young woman with the curly red hair smiled apologetically. "Home." The word hung there between them. Lacey's nose wrinkled. "She left for the airport over an hour ago."

Four hours later, cabin lights dimmed, Joelle struggled to get comfortable in her narrow uncomfortable seat. She was flying home the way she came—economy class, packed in the back.

It was summer, flights were full and the coach section was crammed with people every direction. Babies wailed. People muttered. The man in front of her had reclined his seat so far it practically rested in her lap.

She tried to plump the flat little pillow, not that the lump of polyester could be called a pillow—and closed her eyes. Goodbye, Leo Fortino, she thought, battling the lump in her throat. Hello, Luigi Borgarde.

# CHAPTER SIX

"HE'S arrived, Your Highness." The young uniformed house-maid curtsied just inside Joelle's bedroom door. "I was asked to tell you that Prince Borgarde is waiting with your grandfather now."

"Thank you. I'll be down soon." Joelle tensed as her bedroom door shut, courage flagging.

Why did she wait until the last minute?

Why didn't she tell her grandfather before?

But you wanted to tell him with Prince Borgarde there, she silently argued, you wanted Grandpapa and Luigi to hear it at the same time so there could be no misunderstanding.

There'd be no wedding.

She wasn't going to marry Prince Luigi after all.

Joelle took a deep breath, practiced the words once again. She'd say it flatly, quietly, no emotion in her voice so they'd have no problem hearing her.

There will be no wedding, Grandpapa. I can not marry you, Prince Borgarde.

She'd even prepared for their reaction—steeled herself inwardly for anger, shock. So they'd get upset, they'd talk to her, maybe argue with her, and Grandpapa might even pull her aside, speak to her in that hushed, disappointed tone of his, the tone he'd had when she was small and had broken a rule, but his tone, his disappointment, wouldn't work this time.

She wasn't a child anymore. And she wasn't going to spend the rest of her life trying to make everyone else happy. It had taken that night with Leo to make her understand that no matter how much she wanted to be like Nic and Chantal, she couldn't be them. And maybe they'd accepted arranged marriages, but she couldn't, not if her prospective groom didn't even want to get to know her.

I matter, she whispered, hands growing damp. I'm not just a

princess, I'm a woman. And she couldn't accept marriage to a man who didn't want her for her, who saw her only as means to an end. No, she wanted a man like Leo. A sexy, powerful, passionate man. A man who made her dream.

It's now or never, she thought, catching a glimpse of herself in a mirror above her dressing table—long white crepe dress, a simple gold pendant on a chain around her neck, her hair no longer dark brown but a warm honey shade loosely knotted at her nape. She'd looked just the way Grandpapa liked to see her—pretty, simple, sweet—but she didn't feel simple or sweet. She felt girded for battle.

Joelle exhaled slowly, trying to calm her nerves, and her gaze sought a framed photo on the dressing table. Her mother, the year her first album went platinum. In the color photo her mother, glammed up for a televised award ceremony, was laughing. Young, gorgeous, already hugely successful, she looked like a woman at the top of the world.

Joelle's chest squeezed tight. She envied her mother like mad. *You were lucky, Mum,* she thought, you had everything.

Joelle descended the sweeping staircase, trying not to think, trying not to feel. It was Grandpapa's big party tonight, and everyone near and dear to his heart had been invited, including Luigi Borgarde.

Tonight was their official meet and she found it ironic that he should wait for Grandpapa's party—two weeks before the wedding—to actually meet her. Talk about an eager bridegroom.

She'd known all week she'd see Luigi tonight, had realized with slow but growing conviction that she could never marry Luigi, especially not after what happened in New Orleans.

Perhaps if she hadn't slept with Leo…

But it wasn't even the sex, or losing her virginity that had changed her mind, it was Leo himself. The feelings she harbored.

She'd cared for him. Really, truly cared and since that night nothing had been the same. Nothing within herself felt the same. Leo made love to her so thoroughly, so completely she knew she'd never forget his warmth, or passion.

Entering the Queen's Reception Room, the smallest of the

three palace ballrooms, the white wainscoting and glossy crown molding a crisp contrast to the rich cobalt-blue walls, Joelle searched the room for her grandfather.

And found him. He was standing alone. She felt a tug on her heart.

The five ornate Venetian chandeliers laden with blue and white crystals glittered on King Remi Duccasse in his black evening coat, his thinning hair combed back from his still handsome face.

He was eighty-five and this would be his second birthday without Grandmama.

Joelle swallowed hard, swallowed around the lump swelling in her throat, and as she moved toward Grandpapa, the crowd parted and she realized she'd been mistaken.

He wasn't alone.

Joelle froze, unable to take another step.

Grandpapa was before the massive Titian—Grandmama's favorite masterpiece—and yet his back was to the painting, his attention focused on a guest. She couldn't see the guest's face but the guest was tall—too tall—and his shoulders broad—too broad—and Joelle felt her blood turn to ice.

She knew the guest.

She knew only one man that exuded power. Authority.

Her stomach in a free fall, she could only stand and stare, blood freezing, bones like ice.

For seven days she'd done everything in her power to exonerate Leo Fortino from her memory and yet here he was, standing so casually with her grandfather.

Suddenly the world looked fragile, like one of the delicate blue crystals dangling from the elaborate chandeliers and she realized her curiosity had beaten her this time.

The night she'd spent with Leo in New Orleans wasn't supposed to have left her feeling this way, certainly not so battered. At the time the intimacy felt incredible, but the effort to forget him this past week, the effort it had taken to accept that she couldn't marry Luigi Borgarde, that her feelings for Leo wouldn't allow her to marry another man…a stranger…had drained her.

But part of the detachment, part of the pain, had been accepting that Leo was gone from her life, that Leo would never be part of her life and yet here he was…

Here he stood…

She didn't understand, couldn't grasp how he could suddenly be here, in her world, in her palace, with her grandfather.

But maybe it wasn't really him, she told herself, goose bumps covering her arms, her slim gown feeling sheer, bare. Maybe her need for him was so great that she'd dreamed him up, conjured him like a wizard. He might have the same dark, nearly black hair as the guest, and he might stand the same, but surely there were many Italian, French and Spanish guests, many men with elegance. Sophistication.

Move, she told herself, realizing guests were glancing at her, watching. She forced herself to take a step forward and yet her legs were heavy, her body like lead.

She reached Grandpapa's side, saw her grandfather look up, smile, saw the guest start to turn and shock washed through her in waves.

*Leo.*

It *was* Leo, and he was looking at her, waiting for her to speak, yet she couldn't make a sound.

What was he doing here? And why did he look so angry with her?

Emotion clawed at her, overwhelming her. She opened her mouth to say his name but no sound came out.

And still he said nothing.

Oh God. This was bad, such a mess. Obviously he now knew who she was, knew about her engagement and from the look on his face, from that hard stony silence, she knew he was livid.

She'd thought of him endlessly this past week, and it had never crossed her mind that she could meet him here, that they'd meet like this. It was too much. Her nerves sparked, hot, sharp, and tears filled her eyes.

''Joelle, love.'' Her grandfather's voice drew her gaze to his.

She could barely see her grandfather through the tears filming her eyes.

She blinked, pressed her nails to her palms, bit down on the inside of her lip to make the tears dry quickly.

She could see Grandpapa now. He was leaning heavily on his cane, but his blue eyes smiled warmly.

She forced a smile to her lips, moved closer to his side. "Happy Birthday, Grandpapa," she whispered, rising on tiptoe to kiss his papery cheek. He smelled of soap and lather and an old-fashioned aftershave, one that smelled of spice, musk and rose.

"Thank you, my darling." King Remi slid an arm briefly around her waist, turning her to face the guest. "And Joelle, love, you must know who this is."

Her breath caught in her throat. Yes, she thought, fighting the wild beating of her heart, she knew who he was. He looked gorgeous, too, dressed in formal evening wear, his white shirt a stunning contrast to the bronze of his skin. She stole a glance up into his face, trying to read something in his expression but he'd closed himself off, leaving just the externals, the dark hair, the hard high cheekbones, the full mouth with the indentation in the lower lip.

And just like that she remembered the feel of his mouth on hers, remembered the way he kissed, he touched and she burned hot, burned feverishly.

This is why you can't marry Luigi, she thought, this is why you can't give yourself to another man. You've already given your heart to Leo.

Not that he seemed very happy to see her.

But Leo couldn't be her first thought. She had to remember what she'd come downstairs to do—to say. She had to deal with Grandpapa and Prince Luigi Borgarde first and then she could think about Leo.

"She's beautiful, isn't she?" Grandpapa said, giving her waist another squeeze.

"She is," Leo agreed, but his voice came out rough, raw, and her head jerked up, their gazes locking.

Joelle couldn't read Leo's expression—his features so hard, so stony they reminded her of a glacier—but that glacier cold sent alarm rushing through her.

Head spinning, she looked away, took a breath, tried to focus. But why was he upset? What reason did he have to be unhappy with her? He was the one who said it was just sex, only sex, and she'd agreed. She hadn't asked for any promises. She'd made no demands…

Her fingers curled instinctively, her heavy engagement ring pinching. Did Grandpapa know about her night with Leo? Was he aware of what had happened?

No, she answered immediately, Grandpapa wasn't. Grandpapa wouldn't be smiling if he knew. Grandpapa was as old-fashioned as his aftershave.

A waiter materialized with silver tray.

"Ah, excellent," her grandfather said, sounding infinitely pleased. "Champagne." He took a flute, handed one to Joelle, another to Leo.

"A toast to celebrate my granddaughter's safe return," he added, lifting his own flute. "I couldn't ask for a better birthday present. It's wonderful to have you home, my darling."

Her throat worked. She struggled to smile. "Thank you, Grandpapa." She clinked glasses with her grandfather, studiously avoiding Leo altogether and yet she felt his attention, felt his intense energy.

Why did she ever go to New Orleans? Why did she ever want passion? What was it about fire and ice that appealed?

She'd had the fire. Now she was getting the ice.

Joelle forced herself to drink, hiding the fact that she felt like a sheet of ice under intense pressure. She was cracking, would soon shatter.

Meeting Leo like this was cruel. Brutally unfair.

She'd wanted to see him again, but not here, not at Grandpapa's party, not when she was still engaged to someone else.

"Ready for the wedding?" Grandpapa asked, grinning, and for a moment he looked exactly like a kid—boyish, excited, eager.

"Grandpapa," she choked, flushing.

He didn't appear to hear. "Just two weeks from now. It'll be here before you know it."

"Please, not now, Grandpapa." She wobbled in her shoes, her strappy high heels barely able to hold her.

"No need to be nervous. Prince Borgarde won't rush you. He knows you're young, inexperienced—"

She grabbed his arm, held tight, interrupting him. Her grandfather looked down into her face. "What's wrong?" he asked.

She couldn't speak. Fresh ice water sluiced through her veins. She shook her head, removed her numb hand, certain she'd drop her flute any moment.

King Remi patted her shoulder. "Everything's going to be fine, dear. Every bride feels nervous—"

"We have to talk about the wedding," she said quickly, her voice pitched low. "I wanted to talk to you and Prince Borgarde at the same time, but since he's not here—"

"Not here?" her grandfather repeated in confusion. "What are you saying, Joelle?"

"That I can't marry Prince Borgarde." Joelle felt so hot and yet she'd begun to shiver in her simple Grecian-style gown. "And I don't have the feelings—"

"Feelings?" her grandfather interrupted yet again. "I don't understand a word you're saying, Joelle. Of course you don't have feelings yet for Leo, you've only just met."

"You mean Luigi," she corrected hoarsely.

Her grandfather tapped his cane impatiently. "Who is Luigi?"

Joelle knew they were drawing attention and she lowered her voice. "Prince Borgarde. Luigi Borgarde."

"There's no Luigi, only Leo," her grandfather's voice thundered and Joelle saw guests glance their way.

"What?"

"There's no Luigi," her grandfather repeated. "I don't know where you got this Luigi from."

She suddenly couldn't breathe, couldn't get air.

"And there will be a wedding," her grandfather persisted.

The room swam. The words floated inside Joelle's head. What was Grandpapa saying? He couldn't possibly mean…he wasn't intending…Leo wasn't Luigi…

"I don't feel very well," she said vaguely, legs starting to buckle.

Her grandfather didn't hear her; he was lifting his flute, proposing a toast. "To the future," King Remi said, lifting his glass even higher.

She knew Grandpapa's hearing wasn't what it used to be, knew he turned down his hearing aid for noisy functions like this, but his gesture felt unusually cruel considering the circumstances.

"To the future," Leo echoed, raising his own flute, and in the light the silver gleamed, blinding her.

Joelle could see nothing but the tiny beads of moisture glistening on the lower half of the silver flute.

The future…

Her future…

She shook her head, dizzy, disoriented. Nothing made sense. She felt sick all the way through. What she needed was a chair. Someplace to sit, just to get her bearings back.

"I'm feeling—" She broke off, blinked, tried to swallow and a hand touched her elbow.

"Faint?" The hard male voice concluded for her. Leo's voice. Leo's sarcasm.

*Yes.*

His touch scorched her, his touch so familiar and yet so painful. His touch having turned her inside out a week ago and now he was here, and standing with her grandfather, and making toasts and saying words that confused her.

He couldn't be.

He couldn't be.

He couldn't—

Weakly she looked up, met his gaze, saw the cold fury in his eyes, saw the lines etched at his mouth, saw that she had somehow made a huge mistake.

Fingers numb, she lost her grip, dropped her glass.

The silver flute bounced, a loud noisy clatter, champagne sloshing out, drenching Leo's trouser.

"I'm sorry. I'm so sorry." Torn between relief and shame, Joelle fumbled for a napkin and knelt down. Reaching for the fallen flute, she began mopping up the champagne pooling on the marble floor.

"Leave it, my dear," Grandfather said, his cane moving forward, bumping her hands. "The staff will do that."

She shook her head, body hot, heat scorching through her. "Someone might fall," she choked, her hands trembling like mad as she soaked up more champagne, the linen napkin sopping wet. Oh my God, oh my God…

But Leo wouldn't let her remain on the ground. He wrapped his hand around her upper arm, pulled her none too gently to her feet. "You'll ruin your gown."

Her white gown was the least of her worries but Leo didn't let go, his fingers still wrapped snugly around her arm, close to her elbow.

"I'm sorry," she repeated for lack of anything better to say. "I'm sorry. I made a mess."

"Depends on your definition of a mess," Leo answered, and something in his voice drew her head up.

He was smiling down at her but it wasn't a real smile. She knew him, knew how he smiled. Leo was livid. Beyond livid.

His fury put fresh terror in her heart. "You knew," she choked, her voice dropping, cracking. "You knew in New Orleans."

"Yes."

He sounded so calm, so controlled and she held his gaze a moment longer, sick, so sick at heart.

He'd known and he'd pretended he hadn't.

He'd seduced her knowing she'd be his wife.

He'd played her as if she were nothing. No one. Certainly no one of consequence.

Her hand tightened helplessly around the damp linen napkin, squeezing champagne drops onto the floor. "I trusted you." Her voice, husky with emotion, broke. "I thought…"

Leo arched a brow. "What?"

Grandfather's cane impatiently tapped the marble floor. "What's this? What are you saying, Joelle? Speak up, my dear, you know I don't hear as well as I used to."

"Forgive us, Your Highness." It was Leo who spoke, and although he raised his voice to be heard clearly, his tone was deferential. "But Princess Joelle was expressing her displeasure with me. She claims she didn't know me in New Orleans."

"Not know you?" the king repeated sharply. "What does that mean?"

"It means, Your Highness, she didn't recognize me. Didn't realize I was—" Leo shot Joelle a sharp glance "—her prince."

Joelle's jaw dropped even as spots danced before her eyes. This was madness, utter madness.

But her grandfather's cane was tapping the marble floor with short irritable bursts. "But of course she knew you! She saw you last week in America. You did say you'd had a chance to get to spend time together in New Orleans."

*No.*

Joelle tried to protest, tried to speak and yet nothing came out. No sound, no breath. Nothing at all.

"You don't remember Leo?" King Remi turned on Joelle, his expression almost fierce, bushy white eyebrows furrowing. "It's only been a week. How can you not remember him?"

"I—" She forced air into her lungs, forced the air out again. "I—remember."

"So what's the problem?"

Hot tears stung the back of her eyes. Her heart felt like glass splintering in a thousand pieces. "There's no problem."

"She's just overwhelmed," Leo said, smiling down at her, the same frightening predatory smile of earlier. "Perhaps the princess and I need some time alone."

A shudder raced through her. Time alone with Leo? Time alone after what he did to her? Time alone after the hurt he'd inflicted? No. Never. *Never.* "I don't think so," she answered stiffly, drawing as far from him as possible. "It's Grandfather's birthday, I don't want to leave him now—"

"Nonsense." Grandfather's cane banged once. "You two obviously need time together. Go out, get some fresh air, but return when dinner is served. You're sitting with me. Prince Borgarde is my guest of honor."

Joelle made a last grab for her grandfather but he was already moving on, leaving her alone with Leo.

There was a moment of heavy silence, the kind that blankets all sound and space.

"Surprised?" Leo murmured at last.

Her heart pounded fiercely. She knew him. She didn't know him. He was a stranger, but he wasn't. How was it possible for so much to have happened between them, and yet in the space of things, it was so little? One night. One brief fling...

But it had never been a fling, not to her. She'd felt something for him, felt something real, and yet she saw now it had been a game to him. He was trapping her, manipulating her...sex was just a test of sorts.

Sick, horrified, she turned away, dragged a shallow breath.

"I hate you," she stammered, aware that he watched her, aware that he was standing close, too close, aware that everything she'd felt was false...a betrayal.

"You didn't hate me when we were in bed."

Bastard. Tears filled her eyes and she took another painful, shallow breath. Her lungs were on fire and yet the fire was nothing compared to the blistering of her heart.

He, Leo, had betrayed her.

Holding back the tears, she looked at him, forced herself to really look at him, a slow inspection from the elegant lapel of his black tuxedo jacket to the crisp white bow tie to the hard square chin. Then she could look no further. It hurt too much. "You knew who I was all along?" she whispered.

"Yes."

She took a step away, cold panic giving way to an even colder anger. "You lied to me."

"No."

She pressed her nails into her palms. "You said you were Leonardo Marciano Fortino—"

"I am."

"What happened to *Luigi?*"

"As your grandfather said, there's no Luigi."

"But you—"

"*Your* mistake."

Her heart pounded, she could barely swallow. This was so

impossible, so incredible. "And the Prince of Borgarde title? Just a convenient omission in New Orleans?"

He shrugged dismissively. "You didn't know my name. I wasn't about to force it down your throat."

"Oh, please!"

"Please what, *bella?* What does your little heart desire now?"

His anger carried a sexual overtone and somehow the anger melted some of the ice in her, reminding her of the heat between them. The passion.

"Surely you desire something?" he persisted, and this time his voice caressed her, tormented her.

He was baiting her, hooking her, trapping her just as he had in New Orleans. But this time it wasn't for a one-night affair. This time it was forever.

And funny how a day ago, even a week ago, she would have been thrilled by the prospect of marriage to Leo, it was different now, now that she knew the truth. He'd deceived her. Betrayed her trust.

Her eyes felt like boiled onions. They burned and burned. "I'm not marrying you."

"Don't be foolish."

"Foolish? I'll tell you what's foolish. This. Us. It's off. The engagement. The wedding." She grabbed at the engagement ring weighing her finger down, struggled to pull the massive marquis diamond surrounded by rubies off her fourth finger. "There's no way I'll go through this now."

His hand covered hers, hard. "Leave it on."

"No." She struggled despite his hand, struggled despite the tears filling her eyes. "You tricked me. You let me think…" She drew a jagged breath. "You let me believe…"

"What?" His fingers squeezed around her own, and holding her, he drew her toward him, closer, so close he could bend his head down and whisper in her ear. "That everything was good and beautiful? That you were sexy and insatiable in my bed?"

"Be quiet." Tears clung to her lashes. She couldn't cry here, couldn't cry in public, especially not in front of one hundred of her grandfather's guests.

"You're the one speaking loudly."

"You're the one being cruel."

People were turning, looking at them, and Leo didn't even bother to smile reassurance.

"As your grandfather said, I think we could use some air." And still holding her hand, Leo tugged her after him, through the crowded blue ballroom, out the tall French doors to the stone terrace outside.

It was a warm night, almost too warm and as soon as she could, Joelle shook Leo off. She hated him. Hated herself. Hated that she felt so much even at a moment like this.

"You can't make me marry you." Her hand grabbed at the balustrade, needing the support. "This might be an arranged marriage, but it was consensual."

"Just like our sex."

Oh, that was low. Her stomach twisted and yet she lifted her chin, trying to cling to what was left of her pride. "What happened that night has nothing to do with us."

"No?"

"It was just…a…one off. Something separate. Something that wasn't—isn't—going to happen again."

"I think you're confused, Joelle…Josie…whoever you are, whoever you want to be. Because it was you and me in New Orleans, you and me at dinner. You and me in the hotel room. You and me in bed."

"No. You were a stranger. You were someone safe—"

"Safe? *Bella,* you obviously don't know me."

His husky inflection made her nerves scream. No wonder she felt so sick inside. Her heart raced madly, her muscles coiled, ready to spring. "Don't threaten me."

The corner of his mouth lifted yet there was no humor in his eyes. "I'm not threatening you." His eyes held hers. "Yet."

God, she was naïve, Leo thought, watching Joelle continue to back away from him, her left hand trailing along the carved limestone balustrade.

She had no idea what he'd been through this past week, no idea how hard it'd been to restrain himself, make himself wait. His first inclination had been to hop on the next plane, confront her immediately, demand an explanation from her. But he knew his temper was too hot. He knew he needed the time, knew she needed the time, too.

So he gave her the week. Allowed her to settle back in. Get adjusted to life in the palace again. But he was done being patient, done waiting.

He wanted answers. Josie had broken every cardinal rule, and he had to understand why. "You slept with me."

"You noticed?"

"Not funny."

"Not trying to be."

"I want a real answer. Why did you sleep with me?"

Her eyes flashed, the blue green darkening in the moonlight. "Because I wanted to."

"Not good enough."

"Too bad. It's all you're getting."

She was hell on wheels. Difficult, temperamental, headstrong. And running scared.

"Wrong," he murmured, knowing he had the upper hand. "I already got more. I got the very thing you never wanted to give me." She blushed, blood suffusing her face from collarbone to hairline. She knew she was cornered.

"That's what upsets you, doesn't it?" he continued. "You thought you were tossing away your virginity, and instead you handed it to me."

"So I made a mistake."

He heard the catch in her voice. "Why then? Why me? You'd never been intimate with a man before."

She took a quick breath, her fingers gripping the railing. "Don't sound so shocked. You saw me at the club. You saw the leather pants, the kohl eyeliner. You saw me perform, and you assumed what you wanted to assume—that I was bad. That I had been around the block before—not just once, but many times." The corner of her mouth lifted in a small, hurt smile. "And you were wrong."

She leaned forward, eyes flashing, revealing the depth of her hurt and anger. "I wasn't wicked and wanton. I was curious, yes. And so I slept with you. Big deal."

He watched her stalk away, across the terrace to stand at the wall overlooking the sea. In the background the lights of Porto shone, the old stone and tile houses hugging the terraced mountain slope.

Joelle braced herself on the balcony railing, the June evening warm, the gentlest of breezes catching at the hem of her long dress, the fabric flowing straight from waist to her feet in the soft folds of a Grecian gown. With her soft honey hair knotted at her nape and the gold pendant hanging low, between her breasts, Leo thought she looked like the mythological goddess Diana outraged she'd been caught bathing by the hunter Actaeon. The goddess had a temper.

"Big deal," he repeated mockingly, feeling momentarily sorry for all the mortal men who angered beautiful Diana.

"Do go away," Joelle shot at him over her shoulder even as voices were heard from below.

Leo glanced over the railing, spotted a couple of the palace secret service patrolling the perimeter of the garden. He raised his hand in silent acknowledgment, then took a seat on the edge of the balustrade. "I'm not going anywhere until we get this resolved."

"Resolve what?" She turned, faced him. "That I was more inexperienced than you thought? That you were the first man to sleep with me? That I didn't want to be a virgin when I married? Well, you figured it out."

Interesting. "Why didn't you want to be a virgin?"

"You're not, are you?"

"Of course not."

"Exactly."

He studied her profile, the small straight nose, dark arch of eyebrow, the full soft mouth. She was beautiful, far more beautiful than he'd thought last week. And the photos the magazines published didn't do her justice, either. Her beauty was too warm, too lush for film.

He found himself responding, just as he had last week in New Orleans.

She did something to him that no one had ever done. She made him feel things, want things, and it felt natural. Comfortable. She'd made him feel amazing, made him hungrier, harder, more giving, more demanding that ever before. And he hadn't been particularly gentle when he took her, either. He'd been burning up, burning for her and if he hadn't seen the sheet, and read her note, he would have never known she was so in-experienced. Especially as everything between them had felt so right.

She'd felt like his. Like she was made for him.

Joelle had been unrestrained, completely without inhibitions, stunningly sexy in her innocence. She'd been curious about everything, interested and open and so damn responsive.

Maybe that's what made him so crazy. She'd been so warm, so passionate and yet she was an ice cube now.

Her haughty aloofness put his teeth on edge. ''You don't just sleep with a man, and not tell him this sort of thing.''

''Obviously I didn't know I needed to make a big announcement. Thanks, Leo. I'll know better next time.''

''You won't be a virgin next time.''

# CHAPTER SEVEN

JOELLE saw Leo darken, a dark flush spreading beneath the beautiful gold tones of his olive complexion. His high-handed arrogance made her see red. "I can't believe you're making such a big deal about the hymen anyway," she flashed. "It's just a little bit of tissue. Completely irrelevant to the scheme of things."

Leo swore beneath his breath, his hand snaking out, clamping hard on her arm. "I can't believe you actually talk this way. You'd make your poor grandmother faint."

She tried yanking her arm free. "You never met her, you know nothing about her, and even if you did, she's not around anymore, is she?"

"No. But I am." And instead of letting her go, he pulled her against him, drawing her in so hard and fast she felt her breasts crush against his chest, felt the strength of his hips against her tummy, the press of his thighs along hers and she shuddered at the intimate contact, vividly reminded of everything that had happened between them that night.

He threaded his fingers through her knot in her hair, his palm against the back of her head. "Why did you leave before I woke?" He demanded, tilting her face up to his.

"I told you," she answered, trying to desperately hang on to her anger, to not give in to fear, much less desire even though her blood felt thick and slow, so thick and slow that her womb contracted, making her painfully aware that he'd changed everything, made her feel things, want things, she'd never wanted before.

"In a note."

"I could have gone without leaving a note."

"You thanked me for taking your virginity."

Her face felt hot, and with his dark eyes resting on her face her lips felt strange, tingly, very sensitive. "I said I'd appreciated

91

your generosity, and that you were a perfect partner for my first time.''

"And you signed it, Fondly, Josie." His fingers tightened, his body pressed against hers. She could feel the steady pounding of his heart through his chest, drumming straight through her.

"Fondly." He chewed on the word, furious. *"Fondly."*

His head suddenly lowered and his mouth covered hers. "You're going to pay for that, Josie."

His kiss scorched her, the anger and emotion burning her, and then the anger dissolved, melting into a passion far hotter, far more dangerous than anger could ever be.

It was wrong that she should respond, wrong that her pulse changed, her heartbeat losing speed, and momentum. Already she felt as if she belonged to him, and he knew it, too. He knew he was in control here, merely biding his time, waiting until the moment was right to take her. Possess her.

And fool that she was, she still wanted to be possessed by him. She wanted the hard pressure, the rigid tension, the curve of his lip, the flare of his nostril. He was primal and male—he was hot, hard, everything big and fierce.

But he—and the passion—threatened her.

Joelle pulled away, hard, her heart still racing. She took a breath, and then another. Head turned, she looked to the blue ballroom. "They've all gone."

"We should go in."

We. Like they were a couple. Like they were already meant to be together. Smiling bitterly, she shook her head. "I'm not going in. Give my apologies to my grandfather, tell him whatever you want…that I was sick, had a headache."

He laughed. "I won't tell him anything of the sort. We told him we'd be there, and we will be."

"I can't do this, Leo. I can't go in—"

"Too bad. Your grandfather expects us."

The commanding crack of his voice was like a slap in the face. She looked at him, into his eyes, saw the emotion smoldering there, male pride and arrogance, and realized that whatever she'd tried to do in New Orleans, whatever privacy she'd desired, had failed.

Her night with Leo wasn't personal, or private. Her night with Leo had unwittingly made her his property.

"I'm not going to marry you," she said flatly. She'd spent a week trying to battle her emotions, riding a roller coaster of longing and need only to come crashing into this reality. "And if you think I'm going to go inside, play some part, pretend to be your happy little fiancée then you've got another think coming."

"Not even you would be so selfish as to ruin your grandfather's birthday."

"He'll survive," she answered, cringing at her callousness.

"Will he? He's been very ill these past few months—"

"That's not so."

Leo's smile was pure derision. "How would you know, *bella?* You weren't even here."

"Don't you dare lecture me. You're the stranger here. You don't belong here. This is my home, my family—"

"Then if you're such the devoted granddaughter, why didn't you return when your grandfather had pneumonia? Why didn't you jump on a plane the night they thought he wouldn't pull through?"

Joelle's heart stopped. Leo had to be making this up, trying to hurt her. "He was never that sick."

"He nearly died."

The words pierced her, cutting so deeply that tears filled her eyes. "You're exaggerating."

"I wish I was, but I'm telling you the truth. You see, *bambina,* unlike you, I was here. I sat next to his bed in the hospital, held his hand when they didn't think he'd survive the night."

"No one told me. No one called."

"Did *you* ever call?"

"There were conversations."

"How many?"

The breeze felt cold now and it tugged at her hair. With an unsteady hand she tucked a loose tendril behind one ear. It was none of his business, she didn't have to explain to him, didn't have to explain anything. "I was taking a year off…" How insane it sounded now, how impossible to defend but he'd never understand her grief over Grandmama's death, never understand what the loss had done to her. "But of course I would have come, I would have returned if I knew."

Leo's features contorted contemptuously. "He's old. He lost his wife a year ago. And you needed a holiday?"

"It's not like that."

"No?" He looked away, his mouth compressed, expression hard, unforgiving. "You don't know what you have," he said quietly, fighting for control. "You won't know what you have until it's gone."

Maybe, she thought, but he didn't know everything. He didn't know how the grief had beaten her, worn her down, taken everything from her. He didn't know how she couldn't function in the public eye, couldn't make it to church or the cemetery without the press writing things about her, writing about the poor broken little princess.

And he could say what he wanted about her loyalty, about her devotion, but the only reason she'd agreed to the arranged marriage in the first place was because she wanted to see Grandpapa smile again. She'd wanted to make him happy. Even if it killed her. "Why are you doing this? What do you want?"

"What do I want?" He laughed, low, disbelieving. "I want you, *bella,* to do the right thing."

"And what is the right thing?"

"Honoring the commitments you've made."

Dinner was served in the middle ballroom, the ballroom painted the palest shade of coral, the ceiling cream, sconces gilded, chandeliers extravagant, dripping with gold and crystals. Beautiful soft frescoes in aqua and apricot filled the arched spaces above each of the windows, the frescoes romantic depictions of gods and goddesses playing violin, harp, and more.

Joelle was conscious of the attention she and Leo drew as they took their places next to Grandfather at the head table. Chantal and Nic were seated at the same table but they were at opposite ends, too far for conversation.

A butler moved forward to hold Joelle's chair but Leo waved him off, preferring to do the courtesy himself.

Every head seemed to turn, every pair of eyes seemed to fix

on them, and in the warm flickering candlelight Joelle felt herself blush. "Everyone's staring," she whispered, shrinking on the inside from all the attention.

"They're just curious," Leo answered, bending low, his mouth brushing her ear even as he scooted her chair forward. "They're wondering why we're late, imagining what we were doing."

She looked up, caught the glint in his eyes, felt her belly flip inside out.

Sex, the word whispered inside her. She only had to look at him and think darkness, silence, alone.

Grandfather waited for Leo to sit. "I like him," Grandpapa said to Joelle, covering her hand with his. "Leo is good. And good for you."

Joelle bit her tongue. Grandpapa didn't know the half of it. She'd straighten him out—eventually. But Leo was right. It wouldn't be fair to upset him now, tonight, not when he was so glad that his family, his grown-up granddaughters, were all gathered under the same roof again.

Apparently they'd missed the soup course. The salads were now arriving, small colorful plates of beet and goat cheese Neapolitan drizzled with a citron and wasabi vinaigrette.

Joelle glanced at her plate, wished she were anywhere but here. She didn't have the stomach for this, didn't know how she was supposed to sit next to Leo for the next hour or more pretending everything was good, that their marriage was on track.

There'd be no marriage. She'd have to pretend for tonight, but come tomorrow, she'd sit Grandpapa down and set the record straight.

Salad plates cleared, waiters presented lobster and steamed saffron-coconut rice.

"Enjoying your dinner?" Leo asked politely. His thigh brushed hers beneath the table, once, and again, letting her know the touch hadn't been accidental.

She moved her leg further away. "Don't touch me," she said quietly, smiling through gritted teeth.

"You loved it last week."

"That was last week."

"So fickle."

"No." She saw her grandfather look up, saw the furrow between his brows. "Dear," she added, forcing herself to soften her expression, manufacture warmth in her eyes. "You could have saved us both a lot of trouble if you'd just told me who you were."

"You wouldn't have slept with me?"

Heat burned in her cheeks. She kept her gaze down. "No."

"Why ever not?"

She nudged the lobster with the tip of her fork. "I didn't want forever, dear. It was just supposed to be a one-night stand."

For a moment he said nothing. He took a bite. Chewed. Swallowed. Reached for his wine. And when he looked at her, she knew why he'd waited. He was hot. Furious. Features flinty. "One-night stand?"

Joelle suppressed a sigh. She really didn't want to do this with him, not here, not now, not with one hundred and fifty prominent European friends and royals surrounding them.

That night they'd shared last week had been good. Unbelievably erotic. Everything a first time should be. But partly what had made it so powerful, so sensual was the fact that it was an escape, a night of fantasy. There would be no morning after. No awkward dressing in front of each other. No uncomfortable goodbyes.

She had a fantasy, a fantasy of love, a fantasy of passion, and it was hers, hers alone. "Don't make me be blunt," she said softly, stabbing at the lobster, entreating him to oblige her, remember civility.

His gaze held hers. His jaw tightened. "Oh, please be blunt."

His tone, quiet, still managed to cut all the way through her. They were destroying it, she thought. Taking the memory of what it had been, how it'd been, and turning it into something ugly. But she didn't want the ugly. He'd been so generous in bed, he'd taken her as much as he'd given to her and it worked, that raw sensuality, that hunger. She'd loved being wanted like that, loved knowing that sex could not just be intense, but deeply fulfilling. "Don't ruin what we had."

"It's already ruined for me."

She flinched. Her gaze held his. He was furious. Seething. "It was nothing personal, Leo. It was never supposed to be anything more than one night. I never wanted more from you than that."

"Good. That could have been personal."

His taunting tone brought a rush of heat to her cheeks. She stared determinedly at the floral arrangement on their table. "This shouldn't be a big deal. We both got what we wanted. I got experience. You got to test the wares."

"That's not why I slept with you."

She swallowed, and turning her head, she stared hard at him, stared deep into his eyes. "Are you sure?"

She didn't know how they got through the rest of the evening. It was endless, felt endless, felt as if time had stopped and they were simply reliving the same minute over and over.

Dinner dragged on. Then finally they were excused and all moved to the third ballroom, the chandeliers dimmed in the large white and gold room. Ornate gold mirrors hung on the walls, reflecting light and an orchestra played Grandfather's favorite music—Bach and Mozart, with Chopin and even Gershwin sprinkled in.

Thank God Leo didn't ask her to dance. Joelle tried to put as much distance between them, finding refuge in her sisters and their husbands.

"How was it coming home after a year away?" Nic asked, leaning against her Sultan, suppressing a yawn. She was pregnant again, fairly far along and everyone waged odds that it would be another son, but Nic and her sons lived in Baraka, were needed in Baraka. It was odd, but Baraka's future depended on Nic just as Melio's future now depended on Joelle.

"Good," Joelle answered, catching Leo's eye. She averted her head. She didn't want to look at him. Didn't want anything to do with him.

She forced her thoughts elsewhere, forced herself to go back a week, remember her trip home, recalling the moment the jet swooped low over Porto. Porto, the capital city, was one of the most picturesque cities in all the Mediterranean.

She loved Melio and its smaller sister island, Mejia. Several years ago Melio and Mejia were very nearly split. Mejia would have reverted to French rule, and Melio to Spanish rule if the royal Ducasse family couldn't pay their taxes and trade agreements, which is how the first of the arranged marriages came to be.

Nic's marriage to the Sultan of Baraka had saved their country but everyone knew with Chantal in Greece, married to a commoner, it was Joelle's responsibility to provide the necessary heirs. Laws could be rewritten, Chantal's or Nic's children could possibly inherit, but ideally it should be Joelle who would assume the throne, Joelle who'd co-rule with her husband.

And flying home a week ago, Joelle had told herself Melio was worth it. Melio was still such a magical place, the elegant island kingdom had everything—pretty cities, small villages nestled in protective mountains, rocky cliffs, sandy beaches, pastures, crops and fruit groves—she'd felt certain she was making the right sacrifice.

But now…now…

Joelle shook her head, bit her tongue, anger filling her. The way she felt now she'd rather see every Melio law rewritten than marry Leo Fortino, Prince of Borgarde.

"And you, Leo," Chantal said, glancing curiously at Joelle's fiancée. "You've spent a great deal of time here in the past few months. Any doubts about your ability to make Melio home?"

Leo looked at Joelle, smiled coolly. "None."

An hour later he was walking her up the staircase to her room. "This isn't necessary," she said stiffly, conscious of Leo just a step behind her. She felt as if he were her jailor instead of last week's lover. "There's no reason to leave the party—"

"You were tired."

His politeness grated on her. Joelle dragged her teeth together. "I don't need an escort. I've lived here all my life. I know the way to my room."

"But you're my intended. Everyone expects us to need a moment alone, a chance to say good-night properly."

He sounded positively smirky. It was all she could do not to push him down the stairs. "But no one's looking now. You can go."

"And leave a job half-done? Never. I'll see you all the way up, safely to your door."

"Are you going to lock me in, too?" she asked sweetly. Having reached the top landing she turned to face him but he didn't smile.

"If I had a key, I'd do it."

He wasn't kidding. "You think I'll run away?" Mockingly she put her hands on her hips, trying to make a joke out of it, trying to laugh, but her voice came out strangled.

"You've run away once—"

"When?"

"Your year in New Orleans."

"That wasn't running away."

"No, that was just sneaking out when everyone was still asleep." His dark green eyes smoldered. "Rather like the trick you pulled last week. Leaving before dawn, scribbling a little note." He paused, assessed her, his expression critical. "You're rather good at that, aren't you? Leaving little goodbye notes."

She ground her teeth together, arms dropping to her sides. "Twenty years of education," she said, thinking that actually, running away wasn't such a bad idea after all. She had no intention of marrying him—not now, not ever. And if he wouldn't accept her refusal to his face, then perhaps he'd have to accept it when she was no longer available.

At her bedroom door, she tried to squeeze into her room without letting him in. But Leo wasn't about to be shut out. "The problem, *Josie,* is that you have too many."

He held the door firmly, his strength superior to hers, and simply waited for her to give up trying to lock him out.

It took a few seconds but she finally gave up, abruptly letting go of the doorknob, entering her room with a frustrated sigh. Her shoulders, neck, back tensed as she heard Leo follow behind. Why couldn't he just go away? He'd ruined everything, destroyed even the lovely memory of the night they'd shared.

"What now?" she demanded, throwing herself down on the pale green velvet chaise at the foot of the bed.

"There's no master plan, *bella.*"

No man had ever been in her bedroom before. Actually few

people outside the immediate family had been here. Her room had always been her haven.

She watched Leo examine her room, first the furniture—including the antique canopy bed hung with green velvet panels the color of tender grass—then the photographs hanging on two of her four walls.

The photos were virtually all of her mother, and they'd once lined her father's study. Years ago the framed photos had come down. Joelle didn't even remember when it'd happened. She'd been away at school at the time. She just remembered coming home and seeing a massive canvas of Greek ruins in the morning mist hanging where the photographs of her mother used to be.

Joelle had rescued what she could, hung them up in her bedroom even though Grandmama didn't approve. Grandmama had claimed that Joelle's bedroom had begun to look like a shrine and it wasn't healthy, but Joelle—who usually acquiesced to Grandmama's wishes—didn't this time.

Leo picked up one of the framed photos from her pretty dressing table. It was a small photo, a candid shot, in black and white. A photographer from a magazine had caught her mother half-dressed, leaning close to the mirror, applying her stage makeup. Star's hair was still pinned up, but the eyebrows were dark, the lips outlined and painted, and yet despite the makeup, the hint of bare breasts, Star looked young. Innocent. Like the girl she must once have been.

"She's beautiful here," Leo said, studying the photo intently.

Joelle nodded, unable to look at Leo. Mother was always beautiful, but she knew what he meant. To become Star, her mother had reinvented herself, losing the small town girl who'd known only hard times and hunger to become special. Mythical. But in that photo, taken at the height of Star's popularity, you could see the small town girl in the mirror, the stigma of being poor and white in the South in her eyes, the memory of the river in the curve of her lips. Her mother had succeeded against all odds.

Her mother had done the unthinkable.

Joelle circled her knees more tightly. "It's my favorite picture.'' Her voice came out scratchy. ''When I look at that picture I almost think I know her.''

Leo looked up at her. ''Chantal said you're obsessed with her, that you've been obsessed with her since you were a teenager.''

A lump formed in her throat and for a moment Joelle didn't trust herself enough to speak. That was unfair of Chantal—if Chantal indeed said such a thing. She grabbed a loose pillow from the chaise. ''When did she say that?''

''The night I stayed at the hospital with your grandfather.''

The night wonderful Leo became part of the family. ''And so she confided in you,'' she said bitterly.

''She was worried about the future.'' His gaze rested intently on her face. ''Worried about you.''

''Then she ought to call me, talk to me.'' Not you. Joelle pressed her fist to the pillow. She hated that her family had taken Leo to their hearts, embraced him as if one of their own. He wasn't one of them. He'd hurt her, deceived her. ''Obviously they knew where I was. You even knew where I was.''

''And that bothers you?''

''Wouldn't you hate it if you were never consulted? If people just assumed they knew what was best for you?'' She turned, shot him a hard look. ''But maybe you never had hurt. Maybe everything's just come easy for you.''

His jaw tightened, thick black lashes lowering to conceal his expression. ''I've known hurt, but I don't live in the past. The past has no hold on me.''

''Lucky you.'' She looked away, swallowed hard, feeling trapped. ''You know, Chantal was twelve when our parents died, Nic was nine. I was almost five.'' She drew a rough breath. ''Nic and Chantal remember Mother. I remember nothing.'' *Not even Mother's smile.*

Leo returned the photo to the dressing table. ''Is that why you went to Louisiana?'' He walked toward her, hands buried in his trouser pockets, elegant coat hanging open. ''To find your mother?''

''Maybe.'' A needle of emotion pricked her.

Actually, in her grief over losing Grandmama, she hadn't known what she wanted, she'd only known she had to go to

America, had to go to Louisiana. It wasn't a choice. It was a necessity, as if New Orleans was sun or food or oxygen.

It wasn't until she arrived in New Orleans that she began to understand what she was looking for.

Family.

Connection.

History.

Of course she knew her father's family—she and her sisters had all grown up in Melio, and after her parents death King Remi and Queen Astrid raised them in the palace—but it was her mother's family, the mysterious d'Villes, she didn't know. The mysterious d'Villes of Baton Rouge she needed to know.

But once in Louisiana her American relatives didn't exactly open their arms to her, let alone their hearts. They hadn't taken a shotgun to her, but it had come damn close. Visiting their ramshackle house, her uncles and cousins had viewed her with suspicion, first doubting who she said she was, then wondering exactly what she wanted from them.

There'd been no big plan, and she hadn't known what she'd wanted. She didn't know what she'd hoped to find. Love? Hope? Acceptance?

Remembering her visit, remembering the way she'd been coldly rebuffed, Joelle felt a welling of old pain. They made it clear she wasn't one of them, and yet with Grandmama gone she didn't feel like a Ducasse anymore. Sometimes Joelle wondered if she'd ever know who she really was. "Laugh, but I think I thought if I could find Mother, I might find me."

He didn't laugh. "Did you?"

She couldn't meet his eyes. "I don't think so."

He reached out, touched the top of her head. "Can we start again? Try to get this off on the proper footing?"

She didn't answer, she couldn't. He was standing too close, radiating power, authority, charisma. Maybe that was what boggled her mind so. He wasn't just handsome. Wealthy. Royal. He was strong, too. Physically strong. Mentally strong.

She wished he'd say something, wanting him to fill the silence but he wasn't about to speak until he'd heard from her. And so he stood there, waiting, just as he had in New Orleans, forcing her to eventually respond...even when she didn't want to. "I don't know how to start again," she said finally, standing, hoping to escape but his body blocked her in. He didn't move. He wasn't about to let her go again.

"Why not?"

*Because I thought you were someone you aren't.* Tears pricked her eyes. *Because I thought you wanted me for me.* But she could never say that, never admit how vulnerable she was, how much she'd needed to be loved for herself. "Knowing what I know changes everything," she answered carefully, avoiding his eyes. "I understand your...motives."

"Motives?"

"You were checking up on me, investigating me, weren't you?"

He said nothing and the ache inside her grew, spreading, filling her with utter despair. That night, that incredible night, was quickly becoming so ugly. "You didn't trust me," she continued, the hurt spreading like a dark cold cloud inside her. "And that's why you didn't tell me who you really were, because you wanted to prove to yourself—or Grandpapa or whomever—that I wasn't good, and virtuous, that I wasn't the princess you'd been promised."

She finally looked up at him, her eyes brilliant with unshed tears. "Happy now?"

"No. I didn't want to hurt you. And you're right, I didn't trust you, and I had to know who you were before we married."

"You could have visited me in Melio. You could have given me a chance—"

"I did. I am."

"When?" she sputtered, fury growing, supplanting the hurt. "In New Orleans? Or now?"

"It doesn't matter—"

"It does."

"Why?"

"Because this isn't a one-sided relationship. This isn't just about you, and your needs. I have to trust you, too. And I don't."

He was silent a moment. Then the corners of his eyes creased. "Perhaps it'd help if you'd think of me as Luigi."

He was attempting to tease her, trying to lighten the mood but he didn't understand that she'd fallen for him—really fallen for him—and yet the man she'd fallen for wasn't real.

The man she'd wanted didn't exist.

"You're not a Luigi," she said, voice rough.

"I could be."

He was still trying to tease and she wanted to smile, nearly smiled, but she felt more panic than anything.

Leo was standing far too close. She could see the way his upper lip curved. She felt his power, felt the tension between them. He was merely biding his time, she thought, waiting until the moment was right to claim her, take her, permanently make her his. "No. You're Leo. Definitely a Leo." A lion. A *beast*.

Joelle felt hysteria bubble inside of her. Fire and ice were great for a night of passion but it would never do for real life...the rest of her life...especially if there was nothing real, nothing of substance beneath. Passion only worked if it was based on tenderness...on trust...but she and Leo had no trust, no hope, no chance.

Her gaze searched the planes of his face, the cut of his suit, the hard length of his legs. Beast was right. A hard, hurtful beast at that.

He reached out, pulled one of the shell hairpins from her hair. She sucked in a breath at the intimate touch but couldn't move, helpless, fascinated. His touch did something to her. Made her just want more and more.

He pulled another pin from the chignon, and then a third and finally the loose chignon fell out, her hair tumbling free.

Lifting a long strand, he let the hair slide through his fingers. "Things will get easier. You just have to give us a chance."

"Leo—"

"It will work. Trust me."

*Trust him.* The words were like poison to her.

Yet as his hands tangled in her hair, and he drew her forward, she closed her eyes, feeling his warm breath brush her forehead, caress her skin.

Taking his time, he tipped her face up to his, and then kissed her, a slow sensual kiss that made her tingle from head to toe. And when he kissed her like that, she felt delicate, beautiful, feminine. He made her feel as if her beauty wasn't just on the skin, but deep, deeper, coming from a hidden part of her.

Her eyes stung, watering, and her lips softened beneath his.

If only he'd never kept the truth from her, if only he'd told her who he was and why he was there...

But he hadn't, and he'd burst her beautiful bubble, the one all women have inside them about chivalrous heroes, handsome princes, white stallions, marzipan castles, and happy-ever-after endings. But as Joelle was learning the hard way, life wasn't sparkling ball gowns and fairy godmothers. Not even for flesh and blood princesses.

After a long moment Leo lifted his head. He strummed a thumb across her tender lips. "Don't forget the photo session tomorrow. Ten o'clock sharp."

Photos?

Her brain felt fuzzy. She couldn't recall anything to do with a photo session. "What session? Where?"

"Our formal engagement portrait. Your grandfather said it's a Ducasse tradition."

"Leo—"

"Remember, at ten. Downstairs." He caressed her mouth again before heading for the door. "Don't be late."

# CHAPTER EIGHT

LEAVING Joelle's room, Leo passed Nicollette on the grand staircase. Nicolette, dressed in a smoke-blue beaded gown, her blond hair twisted in an elaborate jewel-studded knot, still looked elegant despite the late hour.

Nic slowed to speak with him. "Enjoy the party?" she asked, smiling warmly.

Yes, if one enjoyed conflict. But he didn't say that, he was rarely rude, self-control something he'd once prided himself on. "Yes, thank you. And you?"

"Very much. I'm just so glad to see Grandfather happy. I haven't seen him this relaxed since before Grandmama died."

Leo really didn't want to hear this. He already felt guilty as hell. "Personally I think he's happy to have his granddaughters home."

"Maybe, but you can see the relief in his eyes. The burden's gone, the worry about Melio's future. Grandpapa has such confidence in you." Nic shifted her weight, protectively touched her pronounced bump, and her expression gentled even more. "We all do."

Nic's words rang in Leo's head even after they'd said goodnight and he'd returned to his suite at the elegant Porto Palace Hotel in the city center.

Standing at the bedroom's window with the panorama view of Porto's bay sparkling with the lights of moored yachts and ships, he tugged off his tie, unbuttoned his dress shirt, and let the shirt hang open over his bare chest.

Nic's voice continued to echo in his head. *Grandpapa has such confidence in you. We all do.*

*We all do.*

I don't, Leo answered the voice shortly, dropping into a chair in the corner of his luxurious bedroom.

Tilting his head back, he closed his eyes, tried to blot out the whole night, but scenes kept popping up, scenes with Joelle from tonight—scenes where she dropped her champagne flute, the moment she struggled to pull the ring from her finger, and then later at dinner when she looked up at him over her dessert, her blue-green eyes snapping with fury.

Everything had changed, and yet he couldn't articulate the change. He just knew that nothing was as it had been since the night he'd arrived in New Orleans, the night he'd shown up at Club Bleu. That evening the momentum shifted, swung the other way, from the realm of reason and ration to emotion and passion.

He didn't like the shift at all.

He knew what he and Joelle had committed themselves to, knew the marriage was an agreement, a merger of families and power, and yet somehow in the last week they'd shifted from the contract—the business of the marriage—to something far more intimate…far more personal.

This wasn't business anymore. And he felt far from calm.

How could he and Joelle marry like this? How could they enter into marriage with so little in accord? He hated tension, hated conflict, had worked hard to keep control, thereby controlling that which impacted him, but Joelle pushed every button, made him go hot, cold, see red. She turned him inside out and he hated feeling this way.

Marriage should be dignified. Mature. Respectable. And yet Leo felt as if he were losing his grip on dignity and maturity. He felt terribly wound up. Out of control.

Just like the kid he'd been. Just like the childhood he'd know, dragged from one end of the earth to the other with his gorgeous, glamorous mother, Princess Marina, the Princess Marina widely loved by everyone but those who knew her well.

Sick to his stomach, Leo lunged from the chair, headed into the bathroom, turned the shower on. Stripping, he stepped beneath the icy torrent and let the frigid water calm him down.

He wasn't a kid anymore.

He wasn't controlled by anyone.

He was the adult now, he made the decisions, the choices were his.

And as Nicolette said, King Remi was counting on him. King Remi needed him. King Remi was old and needed support.

They'd do this, Leo vowed, lifting his face to the stinging water. He and Joelle would work through their differences, the hurt, the disillusionment, they'd work through this and they'd settle down. Everything would be fine. Everything would work out.

It had to.

But the next morning when Leo returned to the palace, dressed for the formal photo session he discovered that Joelle was not yet down.

He waited fifteen minutes, and then another fifteen minutes and finally he asked that someone go check on Joelle.

The housemaid returned. "Her Royal Highness must be on her way," the maid answered, curtseying. "She's not in her room."

King Remi invited Leo to wait with him in his study, and Leo joined the king, but it was a battle to control his temper.

He was losing patience with the absurdity of the whole thing. He was here, dressed, ready, and yet where was she? How could she be so late? How could she ignore her responsibilities yet again?

Marrying Princess Ducasse had been a business decision. So far it appeared to be the worst business decision he'd ever made. He'd end the whole damn mess now if it weren't for King Remi's age and fragility.

Well, that and the unfortunate fact he'd deflowered his virgin princess bride in New Orleans.

Leo ground his teeth together, clasped his hands behind his back, trying to contain his emotion. He knew who he was and what he was, and while he'd never be a knight in shining armor, even he knew you didn't take a twenty-two-year-old princess's innocence and then throw her back at the family patriarch.

Even hard, cynical royals like himself knew better than that.

"Brandy?" King Remi offered, gesturing to the crystal decanters on the liqueur cart in the corner.

"Too early for me," Leo answered, trying to keep his tone civil, thinking that maybe once he'd wanted to be the storybook prince, the one that'd slay the dragon and rescue the damsel from the dungeon, but that was years ago. Back before he knew who he really was, back before he understood the world he'd been born into, and that his heritage, his very inheritance, would destroy him, if he didn't destroy it first.

His family—the only family he'd known—was as desperate and volatile and dysfunctional as a family could be and yet his parents had actually married out of love.

Love.

If that's what love did to one, he wanted no part of it. And love had never been part of the equation, not when he dated, not when he decided to marry, not when he chose Joelle.

He'd purposely avoided contact until the wedding had drawn close. He'd purposely wanted to keep relations impersonal, polite, civil. Leo could do duty, but not emotion and certainly not passion.

And yet what happened with Joelle in New Orleans had been pure emotion, and even purer passion.

The impersonal, civil marriage had become a nightmare already.

"Maybe I will have that drink," Leo said, changing his mind as the king poured himself a neat brandy.

Remi smiled wryly. "She's driven me to drink, I'm afraid. She's become a stranger to me."

Leo crossed the room, took the glass and stood nearby while the king shifted his grip on his cane and eased himself slowly into a leather wing chair.

"I've sent Chantal after her," Remi said after a moment, trying to sound encouraging. "She'll find her."

Leo didn't think so. He'd suspected Joelle was gone…left the palace gone…left Porto gone. He should have known she'd just leave. She was so good at leaving, so much like his mother, the one who couldn't ever stick around and do what needed to be done.

But then, self-sacrifice hadn't ever been part of Marina's makeup.

"The photographer and his assistant will wait," the king added.

Right, the pictures. The formal engagement portrait.

For a moment Leo had forgotten the photo session, forgotten the reason he was even here this morning.

Pictures.

*Posed* pictures.

As if he'd even wanted to take the bloody photos in the first place. Growing up he'd had his fill of staged photo sessions…all those tense, forced smiles, everyone's misery tangible, especially the photos from the early days, the ones before his father and mother divorced, the ones where his father and mother looked as if they would spit nails if they had to smile another moment at each other.

But it wasn't just staged photos Leo despised. He hated all photos, including Polaroids.

He'd never smile for another Polaroid camera again. Never let himself be manipulated like that…smiling politely, smiling cheerfully, acting as if nothing disturbed him.

How ironic, Leo thought, running his hand through his hair, that he was trying so hard to be polite now, trying so hard to be kind for Remi's sake while Joelle pulled a Princess Marina trick, running…avoiding…disappearing…

Inevitably without consequence.

"We raised her," Remi said roughly, hands working on the polished wood of his cane, "Astrid and I."

Remi pushed his cane out in front of him, tapped the rubber tip against the carpet, his expression baffled. "Nicolette was always the handful. She gave us fits. But Joelle…" He shot Leo another apologetic glance. "But she'll return, Chantal will find her, Chantal knows all Joelle's favorite hiding places."

But Chantal didn't find her, and it was Nic who discovered the goodbye note in Joelle's room, and it was palace security, which alerted King Remi that Joelle had been spotted boarding a ferry for Mejia.

King Remi called a quick family meeting. His granddaughters and their husbands gathered in Remi's study. Leo was there, too, but he couldn't stand it, couldn't stand how false he felt. He was livid. Humiliated. He didn't believe in hunting women down, much less his own runaway fiancée.

"Since she's obviously going to the island house," Chantal said, sitting on the arm of the sofa. "Leo could take Demetrius's helicopter, meet her, bring her back."

Nic made a face, nose wrinkling. "Why bring her back? She obviously doesn't want to be here."

"But that's because Joelle doesn't like attention. She hates the public scrutiny," Chantal answered.

"So stay on the island," Malik Nuri, Nic's husband suggested. "Take advantage of the villa there and try to sort things out."

"I've my own villa there, too," Leo said, fighting his discomfort. He found it embarrassing, discussing his relationship with the others, even if they were Joelle's family. His family had never discussed anything. "Maybe we'll take a few days—"

"A week." Remi interrupted, cane banging. "Two weeks, whatever it takes."

"Whatever it takes," Leo answered dryly, his mouth curving but it wasn't a smile. He couldn't believe he was doing this, chasing after Joelle yet again.

An hour later, the sun bright as it reflected off the water, Joelle waited patiently for the little ferry to finish docking.

She loved Mejia, had loved the smaller island since she was a girl. The palace at Melio was stuffy, formal, but on Mejia, life was laid back, far more casual.

The ferry's captain held Joelle's elbow as she stepped off the rocking boat. It'd been a slow trip, three hours by boat, but she didn't think she'd been recognized. A large white straw hat covered her upswept hair, big black sunglasses shielded her face, and even if people did know her, they hadn't stared or whispered.

The wonderful thing about Melio and little sister island Mejia is that everyone respected the royal family Ducasse. If the Ducasses were approached it was invariably by strangers.

Now Joelle shouldered her oversize woven bag and headed for the small queue of taxis. The villa wasn't far from the dock, just a ten-minute drive.

*"Bella, bella, bella."*

No.

Not him. Not here.

Joelle ducked her head, stared at the ground as if the straw hat could make her disappear. What in God's name was he doing here?

A hand tipped her chin up, forcing her to look up. Broad shoulders. Tall, muscular body. The man had no intention of moving.

Leo plucked the sunglasses from her nose. Sunlight blinded her. She squinted up, seeing the outline of him but not his face. "Leave me alone," she choked, gripping the wood handles of her bag tighter.

"What are we going to do with you, *bella bambina?* Hmmm?"

She felt a rush of cold air dance across her nerve endings. "Forget me."

"And what? Break your grandfather's heart?" He made a disapproving *tch-tching* sound. "I don't think so."

They were standing in the middle of the old wharf, the wooden pier lined with everything from glossy yachts to rusted fishing boats and people pushed past, arms laden with shopping bags, beach toys, fishing gear.

Joelle tried to ignore the interested looks they were drawing, forced a smile. "You don't take a hint very well, do you?"

"You'll soon get to know me." He put his arm around her, drew her close to his side, walked her toward a waiting car. "And happily we've got plenty of time to get properly acquainted."

She resisted moving.

"I'm not going anywhere with you."

He gave her shoulder a little squeeze. "Don't be afraid, *bella.* I'm going to be very patient with you. The wedding is not for two weeks—"

"There's no wedding!"

"Of course there is. Your grandfather's not well enough to be publicly humiliated."

The chauffeur opened the back door as Leo and Joelle approached the elegant sedan. Joelle planted her feet, refusing to take another step. "I'm not going anywhere with you."

"You are."

"No."

With a sigh, Leo scooped her into his arms, tossing her into the back before more gracefully following her.

Inside the car the chauffeur drove as if nothing untoward had happened. But Joelle seethed, her hands fisted at her sides, the big white straw hat resting on her lap. "You've no right. Absolutely no right."

"Maybe not now, but in two weeks—"

"Never!"

He sighed, mildly. "It's going to be a long two weeks."

"You're crazy." They were climbing, leaving the rocky cliffs to the greener hills above. Joelle and her sisters shared a pretty villa on the water with its own private beach but that wasn't the direction they were heading. "Where are we going?"

"Home."

Closing her eyes, Joelle pressed a thumb to her left eyebrow, attempting to ease the massive pain building there. "It's not my home."

He didn't answer. He simply stretched, extending his legs and resting one arm on the back of the leather seat.

She grew hot, her skin prickling from the close proximity of his hand and body. "Do you mind?"

"Josie—"

"Don't call me that."

He turned, put his face in front of hers. "I'm this close, *bella*. This close to pulling you over my knee."

"*What?*"

"Maybe a good swat across your backside would solve some of our problems."

"Just who do you think you're talking to?"

"You."

Before she knew what was happening, he'd lifted her onto his lap, and with her short skirt hiked up he delivered several smart smacks to her backside. Just as quickly he righted her, put her back down.

Mortified, she slid as far from him as physically possible, her skin hot, her backside stinging. "I can't believe you just did that."

"I warned you. It's time you started paying attention. I don't make empty threats." His narrowed gaze raked her. "And forgive me, Princess, but you had that coming."

The car trip did not improve.

Joelle sat pressed to the corner, eyes filling with tears as she silently cursed herself, cursed Leo, cursed her grandfather who liked this arrogant Italian so much.

No one else had ever gotten under her skin this way. No one else had ever made her feel so helpless…so confused…so completely off balance. It only took a couple words from him, one long searing glance, and she fell apart, dissolving into a tearful, jagged mass of emotion.

The fact that he had such power over her scared her. Made her furious. And sitting back on her seat, her behind hot, she felt humiliated all over again. *How dare he?*

*How could he?*

Mortified that a man, a grown man, would flip her upside down and *spank* made her head spin. "I won't forget this."

"Good."

Twenty minutes later the sedan pulled up to a tall ornate iron gate. The gate swung slowly open and the car drew forward. The gate closed behind the car as they made their way down a long narrow drive, dense green foliage broken every now and then by a tropical palm tree, the walls of green relieved only by arms of purple bougainvillea.

The driver slowed in front of a broad yellow plaster villa, a patch of the turquoise sea visible just on the other side of coral roof tiles.

So they were still on the water, but on the opposite side of the island from the Mejia's quaint port city, opposite side from her family's pretty villa.

The driver turned the engine off and Joelle got a better view of the butter-colored villa, a mix of artisan craft and imagination, with even its own round tower. Part French Provincial, part Spanish colonial, the villa's gently arched windows were framed by soft green shutters, hand carved beams, numerous balconies and fanciful wrought-iron railings.

Leo stepped out, gave Joelle an infuriating smile. "Coming, dear, for the house tour?"

She looked at him and her fingers itched to take her sandals off and throw them at his head. Instead she managed a very regal slide across the seat and an even more regal rise. "But of course. There's nothing I'd like to do more."

Yet as she stood up, and his hand moved to guide her she flashed him a touch-me-and-you-die look. "I'm not yours. Don't think I am."

The house tour was brief and to the point. Leo did a quick walk through the house, opening doors, rattling off names of rooms—salon, dining room, breakfast room, kitchen—and then upstairs to numerous bedrooms and baths, and finally up another set of stairs to a large suite in the tower. "Our room."

Joelle went cold all over. "Whose room?"

"Ours."

She'd gone cold. Now she flushed hot. Suddenly desperate for air, she crossed to a window, struggled with the sash. But the air outside didn't feel any cooler. Joelle leaned on the sill, looked out. The ground was three stories below, and the exterior tower walls were round and smooth, the thick plaster a wash of butter-yellow. "I'd rather have a ground floor room."

Leo dropped into one of the armchairs in the pretty sitting area. He stretched, folded his arms behind his head. He was wearing a white linen shirt and the loose white fabric slid back on his forearms, revealing wide tanned wrists. "I'm sure you would. But I feel better knowing you're safe and sound in here with me."

She turned, sat down on the sill, tried to hide her incredulity. In the white shirt, comfortable chinos and Italian leather sandals he looked like a man on vacation. A man without a care in the world. "Don't you have somewhere you have to be? A job…a princely duty?"

"No."

"Surely you're employed."

"Yes." Sighing, he put his feet up on the matching ottoman. "This feels wonderful. You should come sit here, try this."

Her eyes narrowed to dagger slits. "I'm not sure what you're trying to do, but I don't like it, and I know my grandfather would never approve."

"I've been meaning to talk to you about your grandfather, but that will have to wait for another time. Right now we're just going to have some fun."

*Some fun.* The words rang ominously in her head. She swallowed, put a hand to her throat.

"Still looking for fun?"

So that's what he was getting at. Her flippant comment in New Orleans. *Girls just want to have fun.* "Is there anything to drink?"

"Lunch should be served soon."

"Good."

"You made a mistake in New Orleans, *bella,*" he added, his expression benign. "There are lots of men who could have given you a good time, but I'm not one of them."

"Obviously I made a mistake."

"*A* mistake? You've made many. You're careless. Reckless. Self-absorbed. You still have no idea what you put your family through—or the palace staff—when you ran off to America last year."

"I've heard this."

"No, you haven't. Your grandfather called an emergency meeting. Asked your sisters to return to Melio. It was the last thing he needed so soon after Astrid's death."

Joelle flushed. No man had ever spoken to her like this. No man—not even her grandfather—had ever tried to shame her, control her. "If you think you're endearing yourself to me, you're wrong."

He hadn't moved, only his mouth quirked, but she felt a sudden rise in tension.

She could almost see a sign over Leo's head.

*Dangerous.* Do not feed. Keep all hands out of the cages.

Right now he might look calm, but there was nothing calm beneath the warm green-gold gaze, especially when one considered that twice now he'd tracked her down, twice he'd come looking for her. Quite the hunter, wasn't he?

"We're not getting anywhere," he said at length, and stood. A muscle flickered at his jaw, a sign that all wasn't well and for a moment Joelle thought he was going to make a move for her, but then he smiled, a cool hard taunting smile that made her want to scream. "Your lunch will be brought to the room. I'll see you later this evening."

"I—"

But he'd left the room, closed the door and as she stood there, mouth hanging open, she heard the turn of a key.

He locked her in. Her astonishment gave way to fury.

At first she paced, her attention fixed on the beautiful ocean and the gorgeous beach just beyond the villa gardens. She thought of all the things she could be doing. Swimming. Lying on the beach. Reading. But he'd locked her in the room without any diversions—no form of entertainment—no books, not even a radio or TV.

Lunch arrived as Leo promised but the housemaid tried the door, couldn't get it open, and apologizing profusely for being unable to serve the princess, left.

Bastard, Joelle swore silently. Leo would pay she vowed, returning to the window to resume her vigil. The afternoon was picture perfect—just a couple wispy clouds high in a pristine blue sky. The turquoise surf looked so inviting, the water cool, fresh and she itched to reach the water.

Joelle leaned on the windowsill, looked down. Stone pavers below. A couple massive terra cotta pots half-filled with young plants. There was no way she could jump out onto that. And escape via the old tying-the-sheets-together-routine seemed ridiculous at best.

Eventually Joelle gave up pacing, gave up fuming—three hours of anger was hard for even her to sustain—and eventually decided on a bath. There were a dozen different bath products in the blue and white marble bathroom and Joelle determined she'd try them all.

She was still in the bath, reclining deeply in the enormous

tub, when the bathroom door opened, drawing a draft, pulling some of the fragrant steamy air out.

She knew immediately it was Leo just by the sudden rise of tension. Energy literally hummed off of him.

Closing her eyes, Joelle settled back more deeply into the tub, grateful for the mountain of scented bubbles. "Could you please shut the door? You're letting the warm air out."

She heard the door shut, listened intently, and hearing only silence assumed he'd walked out.

But then seconds later her nerves started zinging, again, sending a frisson of intense awareness through her. Her tummy flipped, her skin prickled, even her nipples peaked, tightening.

Joelle opened her eyes.

Leo was standing above her in just loose white linen pants, his skin bare, darkly tan, his powerful body beautifully muscled.

She tried not to stare but he looked lean and hard, his torso cut with muscle and when he slowly sat down next to her on the marble tub surround she knew she was in trouble.

"Have a nice afternoon?" he asked, reaching into the tub, checking the temperature of the water.

She leaned away from him as he dipped his hand into the water. Leo checked his smile. He saw the way she was looking at him, saw her wariness, but also the flicker of curiosity in her beautiful eyes.

And she was beautiful, as well as difficult, and her stubbornness, her *willfulness*, drove him crazy. Almost as crazy as the physical attraction between them.

It had been eight days since he'd had her in his arms, her body beneath his, and he wanted her again. The craving was growing stronger. He didn't know how much longer he'd resist her—or the invitation in her eyes. It was funny how she said one thing, the good and proper thing, but her eyes said something entirely different.

Her lashes flickered up now, her eyes, fiery blue green, met his. "Just because we slept together one time doesn't mean you can join me in the bath."

"I wasn't going to climb in." He cupped a handful of water

and dribbled it onto her throat and collarbone. "But now that you've mentioned it, a bath does sound refreshing."

She threw out a hand, straight-armed him giving him a glimpse of her bare, rosy-tipped breasts. "Don't push me. I've had it today. Had it with you dragging me into your car. Locking me in this room. Spanking me as if I were a child."

She'd thrown an arm in his direction and he took advantage of the defensive gesture, his hand wrapping around her wrist. "That was fun, wasn't it?"

"I'm not laughing." Yet, her cheeks flooded with color, and she tugged at her hand, unable to free herself. "You love this, don't you? Dominating me. Controlling me—"

"You like it, too."

Her lips parted, eyes widening, her irises more green than blue, vivid and intense against her flushed cheeks.

"You love power," he added. "The struggle for power, the use of power, even the abuse of."

"No," she protested, but he wouldn't let her escape.

He momentarily loosened his grip, just long enough to switch hands. "If you didn't love power so much you wouldn't fight me so hard."

She had no immediate answer—he didn't think she would— yet he could see her mind race, her thoughts whirling as she struggled to come back at him with something sassy and flippant.

The king had called his granddaughter demure, timid, sweet. Remi didn't know her.

Joelle was a fighter. And Leo was beginning to comprehend why she needed to go to America, why she'd wanted space from her family. He didn't approve—but that wasn't to say he didn't better understand her motivation. "Give me your other hand," he said.

She shrank away from him, leaning as far back in the bath as she could, yet there was no fear in her eyes, just fire.

"Give me your hand," he repeated. "Save yourself the consequences."

"And what? You plan on tying me up next?"

Heat rushed through him, his body responding, growing hard, painfully hard. "Only if you're naked."

She snapped her mouth closed, but the little pulse at the base of her neck was beating wildly.

And while she processed that vivid detail, he fished beneath the surface of the water for her left hand. She moved to elude him, tried burying her hand beneath her, and yet the moment he caressed her bare hip under water she jolted upright, her left hand suddenly free.

"Thank you." He wrapped his fingers around both her wrists, then slid his palms up, across hers, before linking fingers, locking her to him.

Her eyes flashed up at him. Her long hair was slipping from the knot on the top of her head. Joelle began to shake with anger. "I'm not a second-class citizen. You can't treat me this way."

He lifted her arms, pressed her back against the tub, leaving her breasts exposed, the ripe curves up thrust. "That's right. You're a princess. Princess Josie."

Her eyes flashed at him, daggers of fire. "Let me go."

"And if I don't?"

"I'll…"

"What? Splash me? Call me a name? What's your grand idea?"

Her teeth ground together. Her chest rose and fell. "Why do you enjoy humiliating me?"

He angled his body down, his torso stretching out over hers. He felt her pebbled nipples brush his chest, felt his own body flame in response. "I don't want to humiliate you. But I do want you to understand the commitment you made, the pledge you gave me—"

"Our engagement was by proxy." Her voice wasn't as strong as it'd been. It was rougher, rawer. "You weren't even there for the actual engagement. You let someone else handle the details."

"But so did you."

"Exactly. We'd never even met. We signed a piece of paper. Some commitment."

"I gave you my ring."

"Big deal."

"It is to me." He tipped his head, kissed the side of her neck, and felt her body shudder. "And should be to you. Your word…

your reputation…must mean something.'' He kissed her higher on her neck, just beneath her jawbone. Again she trembled beneath him, and he lowered his weight against her, letting his chest press against her breasts.

He felt her stir restlessly, felt her flat abdomen tense. She pressed up against him, blindly seeking more contact.

*''Leo.''* Her voice broke, husky.

He drew away, looked down at her, his gaze sliding down her, resting deliberately, provocatively on her throat, her bare breasts, the swell of hip, the junction where her thighs met. His gaze was so intimate, so possessive he saw her squirm. ''You are mine. Even if you don't know it yet.''

# CHAPTER NINE

JOELLE could hardly breathe.

She didn't want to feel like this, didn't want to respond like this but whatever it was between them was bigger, fiercer, than anything she'd ever known. He destroyed her reason. Demolished her self-control.

"It was just one night," she insisted, trying to clear her head even as his gaze tormented her, his eyes owning her, claiming her. There seemed no distance between them anymore. The boundaries were gone.

He was dangerous, and yet she still burned for him, her skin flushing, heating, but that warmth was nothing like the core of her, her insides so hot and tight she felt sure she'd melt from desire. Joelle pressed her knees together, pressed her thighs, trying to appease the relentless ache.

"If that's all you wanted, *bella,* you shouldn't have given me your virginity." His head dipped. He kissed her hard, lips parting hers, stealing the air from her lungs, drawing her breath into him.

By the time he broke the kiss off her head was spinning, all thought gone, sense of caution shot.

He released her. She didn't move. She couldn't. She simply lay against the back of the tub, looking up at him with dazed eyes.

He made a rough sound, pressed his thumb to her lower lip, parting her lips wider. "Innocence is valuable."

"I'm not that innocent."

"You know far less than you think." And then he kissed her again, harder, deeper, his tongue teasing hers, before stroking the inside of her mouth.

It was as if he'd lit fireworks beneath her skin and she jerked, body shuddering against his. His tongue stroked her again and one of his hands dipped into the water, covered her breast.

She shook with need, sensation, pleasure. His wet palm rubbed across her breast, torturing her tight nipple.

She whimpered at the touch, her skin so sensitive she wanted to lay down on something soft, escape the scraping of nerves, the bite of hunger. She whimpered yet again as his hand slid down her abdomen, palmed her belly before brushing the wet curls at the V between her thighs, gently parting her thighs.

Oh Lord, she breathed in hard, air strangled, gasped as he stroked the soft folds between her thighs, then parted even those. His fingertips were light, teasing, but he knew exactly what he was doing. She trembled, flexed her hands, shivers of hot-honey feeling racing through her. She knew where she wanted him to touch her, knew how she wanted him to touch her but he didn't touch her there, was in no hurry to do anything but wind her up tighter and tighter.

"Leo."

She felt a flutter of sensation across her clitoris, a flutter and nothing more.

"Yes, Josie?"

She balled her hands. "You're driving me mad."

"Then you know the way I feel." He stroked her tummy, caressed her breast and drew his hand from the water. As he stood up, he reached for a bath towel. "Time to dress, *bambina*. We have dinner plans and can't be late."

Joelle grabbed the towel he held out to her, stepped quickly from the tub, trying to cover herself up as fast as possible. "We're going *out?*"

"Yes?"

"In public?"

"That's the general idea."

The bathroom was steady, the bronze bath fixtures beaded with moisture. She pushed a hand through her hair, knowing it'd be a disaster "But where would we go?"

"We've reservations at Henri's."

Henri's was the island's swankiest French restaurant, sitting high on Mejia's tallest peak, with a treacherous drive up the side of the mountain but with a view so spectacular that no one complained once there.

Visiting film stars and European fashion celebrities loved Henri's. It was said you couldn't dine at Henri's without seeing a half dozen of the most famous faces in the world, and the parking lot certainly had more limos and luxury cars than any other lot on Melio or Mejia.

Her mouth opened, closed, and she stared at him perplexed. She hadn't eaten at Henri's in years, and even then, she'd been with family, and to actually go there tonight with someone like Leo…

And it wasn't Leo's title or wealth that intimidated her, but his sensuality, his frank sexual energy…

She looked up at him, towel pressed tightly to her breast. "Why?"

"You're my fiancée."

He made it sound so normal, as if they were like everyone else, a civilized couple—a cohesive couple—instead of Leo and Joelle locked in a desperate power struggle.

"We're having dinner," he soothed as she said nothing, and he lifted her chin, kissed the corner of her mouth. "You've eaten in public with me before."

"Yes, but I remember how this works. Drinks…dinner…" Her voice trailed off, her eyebrows rose.

"Dessert?"

"Of course."

He kissed the corner of her mouth again, his lips brushing the edge of her upper lip and soft sensitive skin.

She tensed at the coil of pleasure in her middle, felt fresh heat and the shimmer of desire. "I'll dress," she whispered, her grasp on her towel weakening.

"Good idea."

He entered his walk-in closet—they both had their own—and she heard him draw a shirt from a wooden hanger, heard the rustle of clothes and she forced herself to get moving.

In her closet she discovered her wardrobe from the family villa in town—skirts, and dresses, sporty outfits and casual summer wear—a wardrobe usually reserved for the family holidays at the Mejia beach house.

She frowned at the clothes, uncertain what to pick, then

reached for a short red beaded dress tucked between more sedate wear. Nic's Va-va-room dress. Chantal used to give Nic grief whenever Nic wore the dress. Nic claimed the sexy bloodred sequin dress was like a Get Out of Jail free card—whenever she wore it, she got away with anything she wanted.

"You're going to wear that?" Leo's voice came from the closet entrance and she spun around, the dress still pressed against her.

"It's over the top," she agreed, giving the shimmering dress a shake, sequins throwing off little rainbows of light. "And it's actually not mine."

"Wear it."

"You don't like it." But she liked the way he looked. He was wearing black trousers, a thin black turtleneck, expensive shoes and matching leather belt.

"I do."

She looked up at him suddenly, struck again by his intense maleness, his impossibly good looks. Tall, dark, unbearably handsome. What had been a blur became very clear. The dark green eyes. The stubble of a beard on his wide jaw. His thick dark hair, a little long so that it brushed his nape, in equally thick dark waves. "You're conservative."

"Not that conservative."

She heard his tone, felt inflection—wicked—and it was like stoking the fire. Flames shot through her, licking at every nerve, every dangerous thought. Suddenly shy, aware of all she didn't know, Joelle put the red dress back and reached for alternative outfits. She held up the first, a simple cream pantsuit. "I know you'd like this. It's Valentino—"

"No."

She presented the other. "Classic black sheath. Accessorized with pearls—"

"Wear the red. It suits you." He glanced at his watch, turned away. "But hurry. The car is picking us up soon."

She didn't have time to style her hair properly, forced to leave it loose, but she did use mascara and a deep red lipstick that matched the ruby sheen of her dress perfectly.

"Ready?" Leo asked, looking up from the newspaper he'd been reading.

"Yes."

"Good." He rose. "I've something for you," he added, taking a little box from the table next to him. Leo took the lid off, turned the box around.

A bracelet. Rich, heavy shiny silver. Caught off guard, Joelle felt something shift inside of her. "How lovely."

"Isn't it?" He lifted the band, opened the clasp and snapped it around her wrist. He squeezed the band and it mysteriously shrank smaller.

She lifted her wrist, saw her reflection in the polished silver. "When did you get this?"

"This morning."

She felt a pang, imagining how he'd felt when she'd stood him up for the photo shoot. "Thank you."

"My pleasure." His hand circled her wrist and the band briefly, checking the fit. "It was lucky of your brother-in-law to have it with him."

Her brow creased. "Who? Malik or Demetrius?"

"Demetrius, of course. He's the one that specializes in surveillance and security."

Joelle felt a chilly wind blow through her. Her gaze dropped to the bracelet, to Leo's hand still encircling her wrist. "What is this?"

"A wonderfully modern gizmo."

Her niggle of dread roared to life. "What does it do?"

"Keeps track of you."

"A handcuff?"

"It's what white collar criminals might wear for a house arrest."

"A handcuff." Her voice rose. The man was mad. Completely, irrefutably mad. Worse. He was her fiancé. Or so her family thought.

"You know it's not a handcuff," he answered with mock patience. "You're not chained to anybody or anything."

"No, but you'll know where I am at all times."

He looked up, met her gaze, and had the gall to smile. "Yes."

The serenity in his smile made her want to scream, instead, mouthing curses, she tugged at the narrow metal band circling her wrist. "I want it off."

"No."

"Now."

"No."

Frantically she banged the band against the edge of the marble counter in the bath. "You can't do this, Leo."

"I already have."

Her wrist was starting to ache from banging it so hard and hot tears filled her eyes. "Take it off. The band's hurting me."

"It's not. You're hurting yourself. Relax."

"I can't. Not with it pinching like this."

"Nothing's pinching, *bella*. It's just a titanium band." He flashed a smile, evidently quite satisfied with himself. "People will think it is jewelry. You did."

It's true. She did think it was jewelry, and she'd let him put it on her thinking it was a gift, a kind of peace offering.

Peace offering.

My God, how wrong could she be? How hard he must be laughing on the inside.

"How can you do this to me?" She felt like throwing up. Shock and rage washed through her one after the other in waves. "How can you think this will solve anything?"

"You won't run away anymore."

"I never ran away!"

"Josie, *bella,* I found you on a dock in Mejia late this morning. You were supposed to be taking photos with me in Melio."

"They were just photos—"

"And they meant a lot to your grandfather."

"He'll never forgive you when he discovers what you've done to me."

"Your grandfather told me to take advantage of the next two weeks."

Heat rushed through her, her skin so hot she felt certain it would blister. She stared at Leo incredulously. "No."

"Your grandfather is actually relieved you'll be here—safe— with me. He confessed he doesn't know how to manage you anymore. Hoped I might have more success than he.'' Leo stepped back, surveyed her. ''And actually, the band doesn't look so bad.''

''Doesn't look bad?'' Her voice echoed incredulously and she waved her arm back and forth, trying to shake the weight of the snug band, the cool metal slowly warming against her prickling skin. ''It's a metal cuff, Leo. Fastened around my wrist.''

''But no one will know what it's for,'' he answered, lips curving, eyes hard. ''Unless you tell them.'' He shot a glance at his watch, saw the time. ''We better go. I don't want to miss our reservations.''

And that was it? she thought, staring dumbfounded at his broad back, the fine black fabric stretched tight over the muscular planes, revealing every sinewy line and hollow. He was just heading out now. Mission accomplished.

Fury rose up, fury that he could be so high-handed, so arrogant, so insensitive.

''I'm not going,'' she said tightly, deliberately reaching for the zipper in the back of her dress. ''You can go if you want, but I'm not going with you.''

''We're leaving now,'' he said, not even turning at the door.

''Then you're leaving now.'' She unzipped her dress, peeled it from her shoulders, kicked off her shoes, knowing that sooner or later he'd turn, and sooner or later he'd discover her undressed, unprepared, unwilling.

Why couldn't she resist him earlier, she asked herself, why couldn't she be unwilling when he touched her?

Because she loved his damn touch, that's why.

He turned, slowly, very slowly, his hard features even harder. ''I'm not in the mood, *bella.*''

''Neither am I.'' Tears of shame smarted her eyes. How could she be expected to marry a man like Leo? How could she live with someone so arrogant, so chauvinistic that he actually shackled her?

*Shackled* her.

Joelle shook her wrist, giving the thick silver band an irritated shake. For God's sake the man had put a GPS device on her so he could keep track of her at all times.

"*Bella*, your dress."

She didn't move. Her hands balled at her sides. "Are you going to force me into dressing, too, Leo? Is this how you imagine a relationship to be?"

He looked at her for a long moment. "No," he said at length. "This isn't my idea of a relationship. I thought this was yours. All you've done is fight me—"

"Because you're overriding everything I want, everything I need."

"You need a husband. You wanted me."

"I did need a husband, and I did want you, but that was before I discovered you were my groom-to-be, and the only reason you seduced me in New Orleans was because you doubted my integrity."

His eyes narrowed. "I was concerned about you, yes."

"And so instead of telling me who you were—"

"But I did tell you who I was. I said my name quite clearly. You, *bella*, didn't know me. You, *bella*, weren't at some exclusive music conservatory, and you weren't busy planning the wedding. You, *bella*, were crawling across a dirty stage on your stomach while men drooled all over themselves." He took a rough breath, glanced impatiently at his watch yet again. "Can we go now?"

She didn't have the strength he did, couldn't fight the way he did. Leo seemed to have light-years more experience when it came to conflict. "I'll go," she said stiffly, "but the band comes off as soon as we get home. Is that clear?"

The ride to Henri's in the back of black limousine sedan was very strained, with Joelle sitting as far from Leo as she could manage.

He was worse than awful. He was a beast. A monster. A *devil*.

Balling her hands, she recrossed her legs and felt the sequin dress move with her. She wished now she'd worn something different, something long and loose and black. Instead her snug dress's halter neck bared lots of pale skin, exposing her shoulders, down low between her breasts, and nearly all of her back. Earlier she'd liked how the rich saturated color contrasted with her skin but now she felt vulnerable, a little appetizer to tempt Leo's appetite.

"You're fidgeting," Leo commented, his voice husky in the dark.

"I've a lot on my mind."

"What are you planning now?"

"All the different ways I can kill you."

He laughed. A real laugh, a laugh that came from deep inside of him. "At least you're not boring."

At least.

The fact that he could even say such a thing at a time like this made her see red.

How could she have ever agreed to marry him? But then, how was she to know that he wasn't a regular royal, but a demented prince with medieval ideas of marriage and motherhood? "Is this common practice in Italy? Do men still tether their women?"

She felt Leo's gaze sweep over her. "Only if it gives them pleasure."

And that effectively curtailed all conversation.

Twenty minutes later the driver slowed in front of the restaurant's stone façade. Yellow light glowed from within the restaurant, old wrought-iron chandeliers just barely visible through some of the windows.

Leo climbed from the car and she hesitated a moment in the back seat, trying to gather her courage, as well as her confidence. Dinner with Leo at Henri's wouldn't be easy. She was already on pins and needles.

But inside the restaurant Leo greeted the maître d' warmly, thanking the restaurant host for the warm welcome.

"It's a pleasure to have you here again, Your Highness," the maître d' answered, bowing deeply. "And I don't know if its coincidence or happy circumstance, but your mother is here as well. She's dining in one of the private rooms tonight, but asked me to let you know that she hoped to join you later."

Leo's expression didn't outwardly alter, but Joelle saw all emotion leave his eyes, his easy warmth fading. He was still smiling at the maître d' but Leo looked hard, granite hard, definitely angry.

Even the maître d' sensed that his news had the opposite effect he'd intended, and with another deep bow, he fell into silence and led them to their table in a lovely window bay.

Joelle glanced up at Leo as she was seated. When the maître d' said mother, did he mean Princess Marina or Clarissa, Leo's father's current wife?

Joelle had never cared about society, had never stayed in touch with the other young royals, and certainly didn't read any of the tabloid magazines that would report such things but even she knew that Leo's parents divorce had been the ugliest—most public—royal divorce on record.

The wine steward rushed forward but Leo brushed him aside, asking for time.

Leo was livid, she thought. Livid wasn't quite right. He looked…devastated.

Quietly Joelle waited. She'd never seen him like this. But minutes ticked by and still he hadn't moved, hadn't even looked at her. "Leo?"

He didn't immediately answer and she waited another few seconds before trying again. "Leo?"

He stirred, body shifting uncomfortably. "Yes?"

"We don't have to stay."

His head lifted, his eyes met hers. His eyes searched hers for a long moment before the corner of his mouth lifted. "I'm not going to let her chase us away."

Her…her who? She thought it was his mother, but she couldn't be sure, and she wanted to know. It seemed important to know. "It's not Clarissa, is it?"

"God, no." Leo almost laughed. "Clarissa's a saint. It's Marina, my mother, that's here."

"And that's bad?"

Leo just looked at her.

A few minutes later another waitperson appeared and Leo ordered drinks, a very stiff martini for himself, and a champagne bellini for her.

They didn't speak as they waited for the cocktails to arrive, but then, before the drinks had even reached the table Leo stood abruptly. "I'll be right back."

She knew from his expression where he was going. And again she wondered, just what had happened between him and his mother?

Leo wasn't gone long. He arrived only minutes after their cocktails did. Pale, his features tight, he sat down, took a long drink from his martini before exhaling. "That's settled."

Joelle felt as if she'd swallowed a bucket of nails. Her stomach hurt in the worst way possible. She didn't understand any of this, wished she knew exactly what was happening, why the horrible undercurrents. "What…?"

"She won't be joining us." Leo looked up, dark green eyes blazing, his temper barely controlled. "She understands."

Turning her head, she glanced out the window, saw the lights of the harbor town far below, the reflection of the moon on the water. It was such a beautiful night. "I don't," she whispered, nails pressed to her palm. Her family had fights…conflicts…but nothing like this.

"You don't want to know."

"But what if I did?"

Leo's jaw flexed. "I wouldn't tell you."

Leo heard her inhale, knew he'd hurt her and yet for the life of him he couldn't find any words to fix the hurt with.

His mother *here*. His mother, Princess Marina, "the most beautiful, vivacious, and puzzling royal of her time," as a magazine had once described her. She wasn't here by accident. She must have known Leo was coming.

The magazine forgot a few adjectives, he thought, biting down, trying to control his anger. They could have included voracious, selfish and unstable.

His teeth pressed so hard it became a smile. He should have known better. Should have known he couldn't return to Mejia, should have known to stay on the opposite side of the world.

Lifting his head, he saw Joelle watching him, her face illuminated by candlelight, her reflection caught in the window behind her. She was worried. For him. And the fact that she'd care one way or another stunned him.

He studied her face, her eyes, her mouth, saw what he hadn't wanted to see. Her youth. Her inexperience. "You're beautiful." His voice grated and she shook her head in quick denial, reached for her champagne cocktail and the silver band on her wrist clinked against her water glass.

She stiffened, and he saw the sheen of tears in her eyes.

What in God's name were they doing? What was he doing? He had a responsibility to marry; Joelle had a duty to bear children, but was this the way to go about anything? How could this possibly be the path to happiness?

Or maybe he didn't believe in happiness. Maybe it didn't exist.

He saw silent tears tremble on her lashes and the tears cut him. He didn't want to hurt her, didn't want to hurt anyone, but nothing was easy, and this—them—wasn't about ordinary people making ordinary choices. Neither of them were ordinary, neither of them could afford to ignore their royal responsibilities.

They were privileged. And cursed.

The difference between them was that he'd accepted the curse. She was still fighting it. She was still certain she could have something different…something more.

Something more didn't exist. He of all people knew that.

But she was young, very young, and in the candlelight with her hair loose, her blue-green eyes wide, her lashes damp with tears, she looked like a glorious Rembrandt oil.

Impulsively he leaned forward, cupped the back of her head and kissed her.

Her lips felt soft, inviting, and he deepened the kiss, needing to taste her, feel her. He heard her quick intake, felt her mouth soften and his body hardened instantly. He wished they could skip dinner and just go home, back to the villa. He didn't want to sit and talk, didn't want to sit and feel anything.

"Let's go," he said roughly.

In the car on the ride home Leo sat closer to her, so close she felt the press of his thigh against her own, felt the warmth of his body through his trousers and thin turtleneck.

She remembered how he'd looked at her at Henri's. He'd looked closely, directly, looked so long she hurt on the inside.

People had taken her picture, waited outside restaurants and public buildings to get a glimpse of her, but no one had ever really looked at her, not like Leo, not with his concentration.

She tried not to think during the drive, and he didn't fill the silence, either. But her stillness wasn't that of calm. She felt wild on the inside. Scared.

Leo had always had an edge, but he was positively hazardous tonight.

The car pulled through the villa gates, the driver parked before the house. The lights were out except for one at the door, and another in the hall. It was obvious the staff had all turned in for the night.

Joelle shot a longing glance at the driveway and the car as Leo moved to shut the door. She wanted freedom, wanted to dash outside and just escape. She missed the freedom of New Orleans, missed being independent and unknown.

But, Leo was oblivious to the tension. Either that, or he'd chosen to ignore it.

He carefully locked the front door, flicked off the entry light and turned on a pretty sconce in the stairwell.

"Bed," he said bluntly, reaching for her hand.

# CHAPTER TEN

HEART pounding she followed him up the staircase to their tower room. Leo held the bedroom door open for her and once she was inside, he shut the door, locked it, pocketed the key.

"Must you lock the door?" she asked, watching him dim the overhead light and close the curtains at the window, the fabric a stunning turquoise silk lined with pale green. She couldn't believe it, couldn't believe they were back to this again.

He was moving toward her, stalking her with single-minded focus. He tugged his turtleneck off, over his head. Undid the belt, pulled the leather from the trouser loops. "Nothing's changed."

Her legs knocked. Her nerves were getting the best of her and she backed up a step, but not very far, and not very fast. He reached for her, his hand on her hip and deliberately he pulled her forward, drawing her to him and her pulse raced, her body hummed.

He was right, she thought, body inflamed, nothing had changed. And her eyes closed as his palm slid up the outside of her thigh, up beneath the hem of her sequin dress. She put her hands on his chest to steady herself as he continued his slow exploration.

He'd found the lace garter holding her thigh high silk hose, and he toyed with the garter, lifting the narrow strap, tugging on it, rubbing the slender strip of lace against her hot skin.

She inhaled, growing dizzy. He was stroking her through the scrap of silk pantie and she leaned against him, her fingers flexing against the warmth of his bare chest. She knew what she wanted, knew how good he felt inside her, but she remembered last time—not the actual lovemaking—but the morning after. Things were already so difficult between them, lovemaking would only confuse everything more.

"We can't," she said unsteadily.

"Okay," he said, even as he pulled the damp silk from her. His head dipped, his lips touching the curve of her cheek as he stroked her beneath the silk again, the tip of his finger stroking back and forth. The sensation was sharp and intense and of course it didn't satisfy. She was ready for him, physically. Her body wanted him but she couldn't bear to feel so conflicted later.

Her hands became fists and she pressed against his chest as hot sensation rushed through her, swamping her, painting stars against her mind's eye. "Can we talk about this?"

"Of course. Talk."

But she couldn't, couldn't find any words, any rational thought. She wanted him, wanted him with her, in her, wanted to be completely his—at least physically—and reaching up, she clasped his face in her hands, pressed a desperate kiss to his mouth. Her breath caught as he slid a finger deep inside her, maddening her senses, making her hot.

He kissed her back, teeth catching her lower lip. She shuddered at the bite of his teeth on her swollen lips and the thrust of his finger inside her.

She leaned against him, legs shaking, threatening to give way. "I can't take much more," she sobbed as his hands took control of her, in her, over her, across her.

He took mercy on her, drew her dress down, covering her lace garter and carried her to the bed.

She felt nerveless, boneless, decadent as he stretched her out on the bed. And as he leaned over her, she reached for his trousers, undid the button and unzipped the zipper.

"I thought you wanted to talk," he said, gazing down at her, his eyes dark with passion.

"We should."

"So?"

"I can't think about the issues now. I can't think of anything but…"

"But?"

"This."

He leaned over her, kissed her and then his hands were slowly moving across her body, down her hips, thighs. She felt his hands slide beneath the hem of her skirt again and deftly he unhooked one stocking from her garter belt, and then the other. Rolling the silk stockings down her legs she felt the air cool her skin, soothe her heated senses.

His head lifted, and he looked at her, expression tense, sober. "If you don't want me, say so now."

He looked strangely young—defiant, troubled, surprisingly vulnerable. Behind his head she saw the sparkle of her dress pattern the ceiling and emotion filled her. She didn't understand any of this. Not him, not herself, not the intense chemistry between them. "But I do want you," she answered, voice husky. "That's the whole problem."

His dense black lashes dropped, concealing his expression, but when he kissed her, it was far more gently, the kiss expressing a tenderness he'd never say with words.

Somehow her dress came off, joining her stockings and heels on the floor. She hadn't been wearing a bra and now she was completely naked before him. He settled her backward, stretched out over her, and then his powerful thighs were parting hers, making room for him between her legs.

She shivered, nerves, expectation and suddenly she felt close to tears again. She didn't know him. She really didn't know anything about him and yet when his skin touched hers, when she felt his warmth, when she pressed her face to his shoulder she knew there was nowhere she'd rather be. How could one feel so close to someone and yet know nothing about the other? How could she want him against her, in her, when he could be so harsh? So unfair?

His hands caressed her rib cage, fingers measuring, counting the ribs and then his palms covered her breasts, her skin heating beneath the delight of his hands. She tensed at the feel of his erection against her. He was very hard, and very big and she suddenly doubted this would work, even though it had worked last time, the first time.

Swallowing her fear, Joelle reached for him blindly, wrapping her arms around his shoulders.

"Don't be afraid," he whispered, his lips brushing her shoulder, her collarbone, the slope of her breast.

It was fine for him to say that, she thought feeling him press against her, feeling her body tighten in response, but it wasn't even her body she was so worried about. Her body was young, resilient, her body could heal. She wasn't so sure about her heart.

But he was moving against her, his weight on his elbows, shifting forward. She felt him push up, push through, entering her slowly. Although hard, he felt warm, sleek, and her body welcomed him, hips lifting to accept him, muscles relaxing, adjusting to the size of him.

The bittersweet emotion earlier was nothing compared to the storm of need, of longing, sweeping her now.

Her whole life she'd felt alone, misunderstood even. Her whole life she'd been the good little princess for everyone, and yet all those years she'd felt so dishonest, she'd felt like a lie. She wasn't a good little princess. She was hungry and wild and fierce and she wanted to be free, and real. She wanted to feel and love.

"Take me," she whispered, emotion drowning her and she was desperate to escape all the feelings she couldn't control. "Take me," she repeated, needing sensation not emotion, pleasure not fear.

His mouth covered hers, his body surged inside her and she forced out all thought but the power of Leo's hard body driving into hers.

Later, bodies satiated, muscles relaxed, they lay close. Joelle was still trying to catch her breath, her body not even close to cooling down but she felt Leo's calm, the release of his tension.

The corner of her mouth lifted. "Maybe you need more sex," she said after a moment, thinking back over the evening. "It'd probably help tame that beast you keep locked up inside of you."

"Beast?"

She tilted her head back, met his eyes. Relaxed, he looked even more gorgeous, his lashes long and thick, his cheekbones high, his lips full, sensual. "Sometimes he's sleeping, which is a good thing, but when he's awake he's ugly."

Leo grimaced. "I'm not that bad."

"No. But the beast is."

His gaze held hers, but he didn't answer, just pulled her back toward him, her breasts pressed to his chest, her tummy against the honed muscle of his abdomen.

He caressed her hip, the curve of her bottom and her breath caught in her throat. They'd only finished making love but he was stirring her again, winding her up, making her want more.

She reached for his hand, attempting to still it, knowing if she didn't stop him now she'd be begging him to take her again. "You've had a lot of practice, I think."

"I've ten years on you, *bambina*."

"And were they all in bed?"

She heard the smile in his voice. "You've a one-track mind."

"Which you've clearly taken advantage of."

"Better me than anyone else."

Her glossy hair fell forward, covering both of them, and Leo picked up a handful of the honey-brown strands, wrapped the length around his hand and tugged. "Most effective," he said, drawing her head back with a tug of his hand, exposing the long line of her throat to his mouth. "I can eat you slowly this way."

Joelle felt heat rush through her. Her cheeks burned hot. "You're not going to eat me."

"Is that a dare or a threat?"

"Neither."

He kissed her chin, and then beneath her jaw. She sighed at the flick of his tongue along her jawbone, and sighed again when he nipped his way down her throat to her ridiculously sensitive collarbone.

"Surely you've had oral sex before?" he asked, his breath warm against her skin.

She shivered as the tip of his tongue drew small slow circles on her collarbone, successfully finding each and every little nerve ending and she was finding it increasingly difficult to think coherently.

"Why surely?" she said, thinking his tongue was awfully clever, seemed to know all kinds of responsive places. "Remember, I was a late bloomer."

"You must have had boyfriends."

"No. I couldn't stomach three-way dates."

Leo lifted his head, looked at her, eyebrows rising. "Threesomes?"

"Me, my guy, and Mr. Secret Service."

Leo laughed softly, a low husky sound that rumbled from his chest straight through her. "I see your point."

"You didn't have security detail on your dates?"

"No."

Leo's tongue flickered across the swell of her breast leaving a damp trail that immediately cooled. Her skin prickled. Her breasts firmed, nipples peaking. His mouth closed over the tip of one breast, and he drew the tight nipple into his mouth.

She reached up, buried her hands in his thick crisp hair, held his head to her breast. "This is getting dangerous," she whispered, her voice husky, and suddenly the tears were there just beneath the surface. The tears felt thick and wet in her eyes. Her heart felt just as wet and heavy, weighted with sadness, weighted with need.

How could she still feel anything for him? How could she imagine she loved him?

Forgetting for a moment whole handcuff security device—forgetting his whole overbearing approach—how could she still be so attracted?

He was tough. Hard-nosed. Stubborn. Proud. Arrogant. Sexual.

And yet, even if he was dominant—aggressive—during the day, he wasn't aggressive in bed. Naked, next to him, he was hard and strong and physical but he didn't hurt her—not ever—not even the first time. His fierceness was tempered by tenderness. His lovemaking had always been intense, passionate, but he'd never marked her, bruised her, intimidated her. Not in bed. In bed he was...generous. Loving.

There, that word again.

But how could a man be loving if he insisted on treating her like a medieval bride, kidnapped, locked up?

How could she think she loved him? How could she want to love him—after everything they'd been through?

It made no sense. And yet what she felt for him, around him, was so much larger than life, so much more powerful than anything she'd felt before. One day she was intrigued by him, the next she was gone. Head over heels.

It wasn't the sex, either, although that was unbelievable. It was something inside her that had shifted, opened, making way for him. She'd found herself in him. Found herself with him. "Did it ever cross your mind, that if we slowed things down, acted like ordinary people, this—us—might work?"

"It works now."

She held her breath, hung on to her temper. "Can we please just talk about this? A little conversation on the topic without threats or talks about throwing me to the lions."

He laughed, softly, but she knew he wasn't amused. "Discussion's moot. We've a contract, made a commitment—"

"Formalities."

"Made love."

She said nothing.

"I didn't wear a condom," he added.

For a moment she didn't understand, didn't see where he was going with this and then it all hit her—like a sledgehammer.

Joelle rolled out of his arms, onto the far side of the bed. No condom. No protection. She hadn't even thought of that. Oh my God. What was wrong with her brain?

Leo rose up on his elbow, looked at her from across the bed. "You could be pregnant."

"I'm not."

"We'll find out soon, won't we?"

Leo's phone rang. He glanced over his shoulder at the armchair where he'd dropped his wireless phone earlier.

The phone rang again and he didn't move. "I'm not going to answer that."

"Fine." She barely heard what he said. She didn't even care what he said, too engrossed in replaying the condom-no condom conversation in her brain. "When did you realize we'd forgotten it?"

He didn't answer immediately. The phone was still ringing.

"Answer it if you care so much," she said, unable to hide her bitterness. They'd just had sex—made *love*—and yet they were back to being strangers again.

"I don't care."

"You do! Just look at you. You're staring at the phone as if it's about to come alive."

"It very well might," he said humorlessly but he did look at her, and his expression wasn't particularly benign. "I knew I wasn't wearing the condom."

She'd rolled onto her stomach to get a better look at him. "At what point did you realize?"

The phone had finally stopped ringing. "I never intended to wear one."

Incredulous she shook her head. She knew he wasn't kidding, knew him well enough to know that he left nothing to chance. If he'd failed to wear a condom it's because he wanted to get her pregnant.

"You need heirs," he said flatly.

Because she was a princess. Because she was the only one who'd remained in Melio, she had to be the one to bring new life and blood to the Ducasse lineage. She had to have children so her children would inherit. She had to have children so Melio would have a future.

A lump filled her throat and her fingers grabbed at the sheets, bunching the fabric in her hands. Again she felt the crushing weight of her position, the weight that had nearly smothered her a year ago when she was grieving the loss of her grandmother, grieving the distance of her sisters. She'd felt so alone then, and she felt just as alone now.

Intellectually she understood that she had to sacrifice personal choice to ensure security for the future, prosperity for her country and people, but emotionally she didn't know if she could do it. Didn't know if she could deny who she was. What she needed.

And she needed a lot.

She needed a strong man, a good man, a man who would love her for herself.

Not for her crown, not for her island, not for her kingdom.

How had her sisters held up? How had they managed to fulfill their duty and yet find happiness? How had they survived the heavy mantle of the Ducasse title—because it was destroying her?

"It's your responsibility," Leo added more gently, as if realizing he'd been too brusque a moment ago.

It didn't help. She didn't need to be reminded of her responsibilities. They were there with her constantly, they were there when she woke, there when she fell asleep, there with every step she took.

The only time she'd felt vaguely free was in New Orleans, dressed in her leather and boots, holding her guitar and pretending she wasn't Joelle but Josette d'Ville—her mother's real name—before Josette became Star.

"We'll get through this," Leo added, reaching for her, trying to draw him to her but Joelle rolled out from beneath his arm and slid off the bed's edge.

"How?" she demanded. "How will we get through this? We know nothing about each other, and what we do know doesn't seem to work." She disappeared into the bathroom, pulled on one of the big plush robes hanging on a brass hook and returned with the robe wrapped snugly around her.

"Look," she continued, and she lifted her wrist, flashing the silver band. "Look at this, Leo. What does this say to you? I know what it says to me—"

"It's just to protect you."

"From whom? From what?" She laughed, a small strangled sound. "Leo, you put it on me to keep me tied to you. You don't trust me. You don't even like me. From the moment you arrived at Club Bleu you've been shocked by me, disgusted by me—"

"Not disgusted. Surprised. Confused."

"Angry." Now that the words had started, she couldn't get them to stop. "You're angry with me, and maybe you have a right to be, maybe the palace PR people did sell you a princess that didn't exist, but at some point you either have to end this—us—or you have to accept me for who I am, because I'm not going to change."

"You don't have to."

"Ridiculous. Of course you expect me to change, otherwise

you wouldn't have done this." And again she flashed her wrist, the band of silver.

He said nothing and his silence galled her.

"You do expect me to change," she repeated, her voice dropping, aching, raw with suppressed emotion. "You expect me to become your vision of a good wife, but I don't know what that vision is…and frankly, I don't want to know, not if it means I can't be me anymore."

"Perhaps we both need to make changes—"

"Perhaps?" she laughed, and jammed her hands into her bathrobe pockets. "But you know, Leo, you won't change, and I won't ever change enough, not enough to satisfy you. And you'll just stay angry with me, and you'll continue to punish me, punish me for being someone…something…I'm not. Punishing me because you can't seem to get past the fact that I'm not—" Damn all, there was a catch in her voice, a rush of emotion. "Not," she tried again, the words still failing.

"Not what?"

"The good princess." Her lips curved but her heart felt like hell. How could he know what it was like growing up in Nic and Chantal's shadows? How could he know that as much as she loved—adored—her sisters, she could never be what they were? And she didn't want to be. She'd just wanted to be herself.

"You're oversimplifying," he said roughly. "I never believed I was getting the good princess, and maybe I have been confused—"

"Angry."

He looked at her for a long, excruciating moment. "Yes, I've been confused, and angry, but I don't believe anyone is all good, or all bad…not even you."

He was attempting a joke, and his expression had softened, but she couldn't crack a smile. She hurt too badly on the inside, her chest hot, blazing with emotion she didn't understand.

Earlier wrapped in his arms in that bed she'd come so close to seeing a happy ending, come so close to believing in them, the possibility of them, but there was too much wrong here, too much hurt. Broken.

He left the bed, walked toward her.

She took an immediate, defensive step back. "Stop." But he was still moving and she extended a frantic hand. "Stop, Leo, now."

He finally did, but not before he was just inches from her. And with him standing above her she realized yet again how big he was, how fierce, how overwhelming. Thankfully he kept his hands to himself.

Joelle hugged her robe to her. "You have to see that this—us—isn't working. You have to see that we're not suitable for each other. I can't be who you want me to be and Leo—" she drew a deep breath, heart on fire "—you're not what I need."

He said nothing. He simply stared at her and she balled her hands up, trying to keep the emotion inside her, trying to contain all the chaos and exhaustion. It was over, she thought, and it had never really begun.

She felt tricked. Flattened. Minutes ago they'd been so close, minutes ago she'd felt so much—felt everything—only now to realize it was all a hoax. A game the senses played.

She'd loved being touched, loved the pleasure she'd found in his arms, but what they'd shared had been just about bodies. They'd have fantastic sex, but they'd never made love, and she'd been too naïve, too inexperienced to have known.

"Every relationship is rocky," he said after a moment, no emotion in his voice.

Her eyes burned and she took a deep breath, counted to ten on the inside trying to contain the hurt. "This isn't rocky, Leo. This is abusive." She tried to smile but her lips were frozen and wouldn't move. "You don't trap people. You don't lock them up or chain them to you."

His jaw flexed, dark lashes lowering, concealing his expression. "I wanted to give us time. I didn't want to lose you, and I thought we needed to be together…to get to know each other."

He'd intentionally forgotten the condom. He wanted to get her pregnant. He wanted to trap her. Not out of love, or tenderness, or anything she understood and respected, but out of duty. The very thing she abhorred. "I think we know enough about each other now, don't you?"

She saw him flinch.

"So why did you agree to an arranged marriage?" he asked, voice pitched so low it was hard to hear. "Why put economics before love?"

Her eyes burned. She blinked. "I did it for Grandpapa. He wasn't well last year. He needed something to hope for, something to believe in." She took a breath, exhaled, trying to ignore the ache inside of her. "How can you even think it was economics, Leo? You still have no idea who I am."

The phone rang again.

Leo stiffened, his jaw tightening yet again. Joelle watched him. He didn't move and the phone continued to ring.

"Maybe it's an emergency," she said after the third ring.

"It's not."

"It's almost two."

"Doesn't matter to my mother."

Joelle felt some of her anger deflate. "Your mother?"

Leo gazed down at her, the expression in his eyes tormented. "Princess Marina doesn't have to follow the rules."

Turning away, he headed across the room to retrieve his phone. "Yes?" he answered, and Joelle saw his already forbidding expression darken further, going from angry to positively murderous. He answered in fast, furious Italian, his shoulders twisting, his body tensing with anger.

She caught only bits of the conversation—basically the I've-had-it-with-you, and you-can't-do-this before he slammed the phone shut.

But even with the phone down, Leo drew short, shallow breaths, his temper barely checked. *"Maledionze,"* he swore. "Damn her.

"I can't believe she's doing this again," he added roughly, dragging a hand through his dark hair, oblivious of his nudity.

"What has she done?"

"Same old, same old."

Joelle returned to the bed, sat down. There was something in his answer, in his voice, that wrenched her and she cared that he hurt, cared even though he'd hurt her. "She's been eating at you all night. Tell me why."

He laughed once, a bitter laugh, the kind of laugh that recognized that the joke was on him. "I wish I could—"

"Then do it. Come sit."

"I can't—"

"Fine. Don't talk," she interrupted, icy sheets coating her insides. He was worse than impossible. He was unforgivable. "It's better this way. I'd rather not know you, it'll make it easier to forget you."

"*Bella.*"

The word was dragged from him, an agony of sound but she looked away from him, steeling herself against any more pain. She wouldn't be moved. Wouldn't feel anymore. He'd hurt her at so many different levels—the dishonesty, the manipulation, the domination—and she wouldn't be hurt anymore. Wouldn't let herself slide back into that very bad place she'd been a year ago.

Move on, she told herself. Move on. Let him go.

"We will talk," Leo said, reaching for his trousers and stepping into them. "But I can't now because she's here."

"*Here?*"

"Downstairs."

# CHAPTER ELEVEN

JOELLE felt a pang—didn't know if it was trepidation or remorse. She couldn't imagine what his mother was thinking, showing up now, at nearly two in the morning. "I'll wait up here," she offered, adjusting her robe.

"And what? Miss the fireworks?" Leo mocked, unlocking the door.

Door open, he raked his fingers through his hair, but even with his dark hair combed, he looked wild, just beyond the edge of reason, and then he was gone and Joelle sat on the foot of the bed feeling positively horrible.

Eventually Joelle forced herself to unearth some slacks and a shirt. In the middle of buttoning the white blouse she heard raised voices. A woman's, and Leo's. They were shouting, both of them, back and forth.

Joelle stilled, fingers clutching the last button, ears straining to hear. She'd seen Leo angry but she'd never heard him shout. When he was upset with her he was quiet, contained, seething. But not loud, not unrestrained, not like this.

And what she heard coming from downstairs was nothing short of chaos.

Joelle cinched her hair back in a ponytail, glanced in the bathroom mirror and headed for the stairs.

In the stairwell the voices were even louder, the conversation startlingly clear. Joelle could hear every word being spoken now and she froze, stunned by the bitterness in Princess Marina's voice.

Marina's laugh spiraled, high and brittle. "You'd have more fun, Prince, if you loosened up a little—"

"Not now, Mother."

"No, of course not now. You don't ever have time for me anymore. You're too busy seizing small countries and adding them to your stockpile."

"I've seized nothing."

"But you're marrying profitably, aren't you?"

"Why not? You did."

The hair at Joelle's nape rose and goose bumps covered her arms. She didn't want to hear this, didn't want to hear another word but she couldn't make her legs move. It was as if she'd become cemented to the spot.

"Prince Leo Borgarde, King of Melio and Mejia. Must feel wonderful."

Leo's silence said more than words ever could and yet his silence only provoked Marina.

"Pretty soon you'll own the world," she added flippantly. "You'll just do it one woman at a time."

"That's disgusting."

"But true. You'll have everything. Who could resist you? You're rich, handsome, titled—"

"And it means nothing to me. I'd drop the title if I could. I'd trade it all if I'd had one normal day growing up—"

"I gave you everything!"

"No, Mother. You *took* everything. Even now you need so much, and I can't give anymore, certainly not to you."

"You don't even try!"

Another moment of silence and then Leo laughed, low, harsh. "You're right. I don't try. I'm tired. Done."

Suddenly there came the sound of a slap, a loud sharp ringing crack that carried into the stairwell.

"Selfish! Selfish bastard!" Princess Marina's voice broke. "You're a selfish self-centered bastard just like your father."

Footsteps ran through the hall, the front door opened and the woman—a beautiful tall blonde in a pale blue trouser suit—turned, glanced up the staircase, met Joelle's eyes before rushing out.

The front door slammed shut. Joelle couldn't move, shell-shocked. She'd had fights with her own family, but never anything like that, never such anger, or hatred, never such violent emotion.

Leo appeared in the entry hall. His dark head was bowed,

expression blank and then lifting his head he spotted her on the staircase. "You missed Mother."

Joelle's chest tightened. "Actually I got a glimpse of her."

"She's brilliant with exits, isn't she?"

And entrances, Joelle silently added, overwhelmed. But this stage drama wasn't new to Leo, she thought, seeing the pinched lines at his eyes and mouth. This was very familiar territory. "What just happened here?"

"The usual."

She stared at him a long moment, knowing there was a dozen different emotions going through him and knowing he had no intention of talking about any of them.

"I don't understand you," she said, feeling cold on the inside, but if it was fear, she wasn't about to give in to it. Fear was something she'd been taught to resist, to overcome with action. Decision. The Ducasses couldn't afford to be helpless. As royals, they were leaders. Role models. A Ducasse princess couldn't quit and wasn't allowed to fail.

"And understanding me will accomplish what?"

Anger swept through her. "In the event I am pregnant, and in the event we're forced to marry, I'd like to know something about my baby's father."

A shadow of emotion flickered over his face. Sighing, he switched on the hallway light. "We can talk as we eat."

And he led the way past the stairs, down a narrow hallway to the spacious kitchen at the end.

In the large old-fashioned kitchen with its beamed ceiling and tiled counters and floor, he set to work cracking and whisking eggs, melting butter in a sauté pan, chopping herbs.

He'd directed her to a wicker stool at the edge of the prep counter and she sat there, out of his way, and yet she watched him intently, studying the hardness of his cheekbones, and the press of his full firm lips, anything to keep from looking at the red mark on his cheek from where Princess Marina had slapped him.

But as he reached for the cheese grater his head turned and she saw the mark, the outline of fingers and palm and she felt the cold stunned feeling return, that panic and fear she'd felt when Marina had lashed out at Leo. But it wasn't just Marina's angry words that had sent shock waves through Joelle, it'd been the fact that Marina had hit Leo. Hit him and then walked out.

How could anybody do that? How could any mother treat her own that way?

The lump returned to Joelle's throat. "Your mother *slapped* you." The words came out in a rush, unable to hold them back any longer.

Leo lifted his head, looked at her. His expression was perfectly blank. "I've been hurt far worse," he answered calmly, dumping the grated cheese onto the cooking egg mixture yet she saw the muscle pull at his jawbone, saw the tension return to his face.

He dished the omelet, having cut it in half and he handed her a plate with her half of the omelet and a slice of buttered toast.

"Taste okay?" he asked, taking a stool across from her.

She nodded, swallowed. It tasted fine, and she'd been hungry, but it was much harder eating than she expected. She felt utterly wretched. She'd wanted to be the good granddaughter for her grandfather, she'd wanted to do her part for Melio, she'd wanted her sisters proud. Joelle wasn't going to marry Leo. Nothing would be as the family hoped.

She and Leo struggled to eat, both picking halfheartedly at their meal. Leo finished first, pushed his plate away, stared at his plate.

Although his black lashes were lowered, she had the feeling he wasn't seeing anything, but thinking. And the thoughts seemed dark, tortured. Joelle shot him a worried glance as she continued to work on what was left of her dinner although after another minute swallowing became impossible.

She set her fork down. "I'm worried...about you."

"Don't." He grimaced, wearily ran a hand through his hair, messing the dark strands. "This is nothing."

But the accusations...the resentment...the anger...how could he say it was nothing? There was obviously so much pain between the two of them and Joelle drew a slow breath trying to find a voice to voice her concerns. "But your mother hit you... She hit you as if it were nothing."

"She was frustrated." He smiled but the expression in his eyes grew bleak. "Patience has never been one of her virtues."

His misery was palpable and it washed over Joelle in waves. She realized Leo didn't enjoy conflict at all. He probably never had. "What did she want tonight?"

"I don't know. I never really know… I don't think even she knows. She gets this way sometimes—manic, I suppose you'd call it—and suddenly she wants and needs everything, and doesn't know how to get it."

Tears pricked the back of her eyes. "So she strikes out at you?"

"She strikes out at whoever stands in the way." He looked at her, smiled crookedly. "But I'm probably her favorite target. I'm easy."

Silence hung in the kitchen and then Leo pushed back from the counter, his stool scraping the floor. Quickly he stacked their plates and carried the dishes to the sink where he rinsed them.

Turning around he faced Joelle. "Coffee?"

She sensed he needed a job, something to keep him busy and she nodded. "Please."

It took him a few minutes to make the espresso and when he returned with coffee and biscuits, Leo's hard mask, the stony one, the one without emotion, had slipped back into place.

"I'll tell you a story," he said, sitting down again across from her. He leaned on the counter, elbows braced, shoulders broad. "But you have to promise not to say anything afterward."

She couldn't help the arch of her eyebrows. "I can't say anything?"

"No. I'll tell you this story, but when it's over, it's over, and I don't want any questions or comments, nothing to embarrass me, nothing that will require sympathy from you."

She hesitated, lifted her coffee, blew gently on the steam. "That doesn't sound very fair."

"Life's not fair."

"No, life's dog-eat-dog," she flashed, "But it's just you and me here and you can't offer to tell someone something, and then put stipulations—"

"But it's exactly what I'm doing."

She set her coffee down, stared at him, not understanding him, not understanding anything about him. What motivated him. What emotions mattered. What he wanted out of life.

He was so complicated, too complicated. All along she'd thought his silence and hard edges were arrogance, the arrogance that came from a life of power and affluence, but she was beginning to see there was more here than arrogance. There was a great deal of pain.

Leo intentionally didn't let others in. Leo didn't want anyone close. And Joelle flashed to Chantal, flashed to Chantal's years in La Croix, the terrible mistreatment she'd experienced there with her first husband and in-laws.

"Okay," she said, "tell me your story. I promise I won't say a word when you're through."

"Where to start?" he asked, and then fell silent. It seemed as if he didn't have the words after all. And then he started in, just started talking, quietly, clearly, as if determined to just get the story over with. "My parents separated early. For reasons I won't go into, it was decided I was better off with my mother. I didn't see my father often after that."

"But you're close to him now—"

Leo gave her a long, hard look.

She felt a funny knot in her stomach. "No questions, no comments. Right. Sorry."

"My mother didn't like being on her own. She's not good at being alone. But Mother, being Mother, doesn't behave like other people, nor does she make choices that others might make.

"So we traveled constantly—all over the world. She attempted to make new friendships—liaisons, if you will—and sometimes she was successful and sometimes she wasn't. But the instability of it all wore on her. She's a beautiful woman, knew she was a beautiful woman, and she couldn't be in, be alone on a Saturday night. She'd be almost desperate to be out on a Saturday, desperate to not miss anything."

The corner of his mouth curved in a grim smile of remembrance. "It was even worse if she had to be alone with me," he added after a moment. "I don't think she thought she was cruel. She was just determined."

"We had a little game we played," he continued. "It went like this. We'd both dress up. Put on our best. And we'd set out, like we're on a date. Mother and me. We'd go somewhere nice—ultra-trendy restaurant, luxury hotel, someplace where handsome, wealthy men would go—and we'd go inside, holding hands, and Mother would squeeze my hand, smile down at me. I was her man. Her favorite man."

He looked away, stared across the kitchen, overhead lights gleaming down on limestone tiles and stainless steel. "I loved that part of our nights. I loved it when she held my hand. She'd bend her head, press kisses to my face and her blond hair would envelop me, and she smelled lovely. Sweet. Like gardenias and roses and no one was more beautiful than Mother heading out for a big night."

His lips twisted again, the mockery sharper, the pain deeper. He hated what he was telling her and yet Joelle sensed that now that he'd begun, he wasn't going to stop until he'd told everything.

"Inside the club or restaurant lounge Mother would sort of scope it out. She'd look for the best tables—and that meant tables with optimum visibility—since the whole point of our going out was to see and be seen. And for a little bit, Mother would be content to wait for one of these popular tables to open up, but if nothing seemed to be happening, she'd start working it harder." He laughed roughly. "Holding my hand, she'd take me from table to table, and she'd ask if we could have the table—"

"Have the table?" Joelle couldn't help interrupting. "As in, take it from them?"

His sardonic smile said everything. "Because it was my birthday, you see. And that's when I was pushed to the front, introduced. Her five-year-old. Her six-year-old. Her seven-year-old. And so on. For years we played this game. Sometimes people actually gave up their table to us, other times Mother was asked to move on, but Mother never gave up. I have to hand it to her. She'd find a spot at the bar, leaving me on a seat outside the door, close enough she could see me, but looking far more available than when she had a seven-year-old boy at her elbow."

Joelle was beginning to feel sick. Truly sick. She rather hoped Leo would stop talking, couldn't imagine anyone taking her child to an adult venue and abandoning the child outside.

"Being Saturday nights, they were long nights. We wouldn't arrive until eight or nine. We'd usually stay until midnight—or someone offered to take Mother home. But there were a lot of hours between Mother getting the good table, and Mother finding her mate. And sometimes she'd get so engrossed in a conversation she'd forget I was there."

He tapped his fingers on the counter, tapped to a memory in his head. "I could be outside for hours. Three, four. Inevitably someone took pity on me, inevitably some woman—probably a mother herself, or an older man who'd become a grandfather and couldn't fathom his own grandchildren being neglected— would bring me to their table."

His mouth curved. "That's when Mother would remember me—always in time—just before the restaurant or hotel manager was summoned—and she'd smile gaily, as if everything was just wonderful, and life was a delicious adventure, and she was so grateful someone had taken time to speak to me, especially since it was my birthday."

Joelle's eyes held his, her heart thudding uncomfortably hard. Each of his words seemed to hurt her worse. "You had a lot of birthdays," she said, unable to say nothing despite her promises made.

"Hundreds every year."

Silence fell. Joelle gripped the sides of her stool, the pads of her fingers pressed to the rattan and wood. How could any mother be so callous? So calculating?

Princess Marina was desperate, Joelle silently answered, trying to somehow justify his mother's actions. But the depths of the desperation…the inability to shield one's child, protect and provide boggled her mind.

Her own mother had been so different. Her own mother had fought tooth and nail to provide. Her mother gave up everything—career, identity, culture and country—to provide stability for her children.

"Did you get cakes?" she whispered, trying to hold back the tears, trying to find something positive to latch on to.

"And pastries, tarts, ice cream. Everything arrived with blazing candles, of course. And these nice strangers, these good awkward, uncomfortable people, would sing to me. They clapped when I blew out my candles, and some kindhearted person—I never knew which—would take my picture, my own Polaroid, so I wouldn't forget my special day."

"It's awful."

"What's awful is how these people looked at my mother. I saw how they looked at her. Understood it. At least after the first couple of years. Early on?" His shoulders shifted. "Who knows?"

He fell silent, and after all the talk, the kitchen seemed unnaturally still.

Joelle felt as if someone had let loose a hundred butterflies in her chest, and their wings felt like razor blades, beating at her heart. "Leo."

He shook his head, smiled, and yet there was a sheen in his eyes, a hint of tears he never let himself cry.

"Let me see your hand," he said, and he took her wrist, unlocked the silver band and tossed it across the kitchen into the waste bin. "That's not necessary anymore."

With the removal of the silver band, her wrist felt light, free, and she rubbed her skin. There was no mark on her wrist, no sign that it had ever been there, and yet they both knew. They both understood.

He was letting her go.

He knew it was over now, too.

"I'm sorry," he said roughly. "Forgive me."

Her eyes burned, hot, scalding. She blinked, nodded. "I understand."

"You deserve better. You deserve someone that will love you properly. Kindly." He grimaced. "I'm not a kind man."

Could he mash her heart any harder? Could he notch the pain any higher? "We are what we are," she said, looking away, fighting tears, fighting herself. She was torn between wanting to tell him that maybe they could try again, maybe they could start over, and knowing they both had needs the other couldn't meet.

He didn't trust her, probably wouldn't ever be able to trust her, and she quite frankly, didn't trust him.

And yet knowing that it was over, knowing that she could get up and go, she couldn't leave, at least not yet.

"Let's get some air," Leo said, pushing his stool back. "We could head to the beach."

Joelle wasn't wearing a watch yet knew it had to be close to three in the morning. Although late, a walk sounded infinitely better than tossing and turning in bed.

Leaving the kitchen Leo wondered why he'd been so compelled to tell her everything. He'd certainly never talked about his past before, had never told anyone about life with his mother, and yet he'd told Joelle everything. Each ugly, sordid little detail.

He'd lost control again, he thought, as they walked through the lower garden down toward the beach. He never used to lose control. Until the last couple of weeks he'd been the master of calm.

Even at three-thirty in the morning, the air was warm, almost balmy, and reaching the beach Leo headed straight for the surf. Already barefoot he walked into the water, let the cool tide slap his ankles and cover his feet.

Jesus, he was like a bleeding, gaping wound all of a sudden. Feeling too much. Thinking too much.

He shoved his hands into his pockets, stared out over the water. Clouds had partially obscured the moon. He couldn't see much and yet he felt everything. Amazing, he thought, shoving his hands deeper. You spend fifteen, twenty years suppressing the hurt, and then in just a few days it backfires. The lot of it blows up in your face.

"Children are so goddamn obliging," he said quietly, without looking at Joelle. He was tired, truly tired, and he wondered how it had all gone so wrong. Years ago, after he'd escaped to boarding school, and then university, he'd vowed he'd never be vulnerable again. He'd never let anyone close to him again. And he'd succeeded—brilliantly—until now.

He wasn't supposed to fall in love with Joelle. He'd gone the arranged marriage route precisely because he didn't want to love.

He'd wanted a wife that was strictly business, a steady, intelligent wife who understood the responsibilities of being royal. One that was ready to settle down and start a family. And he'd been assured by King Remi that Joelle was the perfect princess, calling her the ''jewel of his heart.'' According to Remi, the young princess was everything he required—intelligent, stable, a contented homebody.

Leo shot Joelle a wry glance now. Intelligent yes, fairly stable, a homebody, no.

But he was falling in love with her anyway, and Remi had been right about one thing—she was a jewel. Joelle reminded Leo of an exquisite ruby—rich, fiery, passionate, full of light. Her flaws didn't even diminish her beauty. Her flaws made her more rare. He saw the world differently through her eyes, saw things he'd never seen before and somehow he found himself needing…wanting…loving.

The loving broke him, loving her broke him open and he couldn't handle it. Wasn't prepared for such intense emotion. The intensity unhinged Leo. He cared for her, really cared for her, and the caring filled him with fear. And anger.

So he'd done what his mother used to do. He'd tried to trap Joelle to him, chained her to him, used guilt…intimidation…whatever method he could.

''Of all the princesses on the market, why did you pick me?'' Joelle turned to look at him and the dim moonlight just barely lit her face.

She'd never looked more beautiful, more honest or natural. And he realized all over again what a mistake he'd made. Joelle had never been like his mother. She wasn't flighty, needy, she was just young. She'd grown up sheltered by her family in the palace, had grown up in her sisters' shadows, and she'd never had time to be her own person. To be her own woman.

He understood now how much he—and even her grandfather—had rushed her, pushed her, forcing their own needs on her.

No wonder Joelle had run away. He would have run away,

too. In fact, he did. He'd run from his family, put as much distance between him and his mother—even his father—trying to keep the pain away.

He groaned inwardly, feeling hard, cruel. "You were a perfect addition to my empire." It seemed surreal now to think he'd wanted her for her title, her bloodline, her country, but that's exactly why he'd wanted her.

"Melio," she said.

"It's an incredible country. I've always felt an affinity for the people...the landscape." Since his family's political exile from Italy, he'd had no country to call home, and having spent summer holidays on Mejia, he'd always been fond of the sister islands, could see himself settled in Melio, see a future there.

"What happens to your empire now?"

"It gets scaled back."

"I'm sorry."

"Don't be. It's better this way."

Is it? Joelle wondered, bending down to touch the water. She'd needed a husband. Melio needed a wedding. In so many ways Leo could have been the right prince, the proper fit.

At twenty-two she didn't know if she'd ever meet anyone like Leo again, a man who made her feel so alive, so aware, a man who made her feel incredibly beautiful in bed. But she couldn't build a future on great sex, nor could she risk building a future on what she and Leo had now. With the wedding only two weeks away she knew there wasn't the necessary time to get to know Leo properly, to have the kind of relationship she wanted to make a happy, healthy marriage possible.

And as impossible as it sounded, as romantic and implausible, she wanted a marriage like her parents, she wanted the same kind of relationship they'd had. Her mother might have been the famous Star, but from everything she'd ever heard, her father had such a good, strong heart. Her father had loved her mother— for who she was, not who he thought she should be.

Joelle longed for that kind of acceptance. "Did you ever meet my parents?" she asked, realizing that Leo might have perhaps crossed paths with them at some point in his life.

"No." He hesitated. "But I attended their funeral."

The admission knocked the air out of her lungs and she took a quick breath, eyes stinging. "I don't remember the funeral."

"You were only four."

She shrugged uncomfortably. "But they were my parents. You'd think I'd have some memory." She didn't remember the real them, just the faces from magazines, the photos, the stories. Her parents, Julien and Star, were like beautiful people in a fairy tale. Girl from poor part of town meets handsome prince and they run off together—no regrets, no doubts—three daughters later and they're still happy ever after.

Joelle drew a breath, ignored the tenderness in her chest. She wished she were Nic or Chantal. They at least had real memories of Mother and Father. They had something to cling to. Joelle just had photos. And the stories others told.

She felt Leo's sympathy, found it excruciating after everything they'd been through tonight. "It was a long time ago." She wrapped her arms around her middle, hem of trousers soaked, body cold, suddenly brutally tired. "Shall we call it a night?"

Returning to the bedroom there was a moment of strained silence where Joelle and Leo just looked at each other, both knowing they'd reached the end and it was a matter of formalities. Civilities. Cleanup, she thought, trying to keep a stiff upper lip.

So do it fast, she told herself. Get it over with. Leo would let her leave. He wouldn't say a thing, in fact, he'd probably be relieved, but he didn't suggest it and as they stood there looking at each other, need and hunger flaring, she wasn't about to offer.

"Can I stay the night?" she asked, knowing dawn would be breaking soon.

"You mean stay until morning?" He moved toward her, took her by the hip, walked her toward him. "You know how men feel about that sort of thing. Smacks of commitment."

"And men are so commitment-phobic."

"Indeed."

She was fighting tears, fighting them tooth and nail. "Will we ever see each other again?"

He clasped her face, thumbs stroking her cheeks and as his

head dipped, whispered, "Maybe," he said softly, before covering her mouth with his.

The kiss was unlike any kiss she'd ever known. It was sweetness and longing, innocence and heartbreak and she felt tears burn beneath her eyelids. They'd come so close to something so beautiful. Perhaps if timing had been different, perhaps if they'd met when they were older…wiser…perhaps if they'd met the way other people did, at a restaurant or club, or introduced by friends…

Joelle wrapped her arms around his neck, held him close, closer, held him trying to remember every second of this last night.

In bed they made love, slowly, leisurely, desperation gone, leaving only pleasure. Leo held himself back for hours, building, extending sensation, both determined to make their time together mean something. It wasn't about sex, Joelle thought, climaxing a second time, burying her face against Leo's warm solid chest. It was about their hearts, about breaking them and trying to patch them together again.

Joelle didn't remember falling asleep. She'd been in his arms, her face damp with tears, lips pressed to his chest, and now she was awake. Alone.

Sitting up, she swung her feet around and tried to stand, her chest feeling as if it'd burst from pain. Something had happened. Something bad. Then she realized what it was. Leo's things were gone.

He'd left while she was sleeping.

It didn't take long to find the note he'd left for her. He'd taken a page from her book, used her favorite means of communication and the tears fell as she read and reread the few, brief words.

*Bella, The world is yours. Leo*

# CHAPTER TWELVE

*New Orleans, Louisiana*

"HE LEFT a note and that was it?" Lacey repeated incredulously.

"That was it." Joelle leaned back in her chair on the balcony of her and Lacey's French Quarter apartment and stared hard at the beer bottle she was holding, inspecting the label as if it were the most fascinating thing on earth.

She'd been back in New Orleans just a day but planned to stay indefinitely and if she was going to stay, she needed to get through this part, needed to get all the explanations done and out of the way.

"How do you feel?" Lacey persisted.

For a split second Joelle's eyes burned and her throat sealed closed and then she forced herself to breathe. To keep breathing. "Like hell."

Lacey exhaled in a whoosh of air. "I'm sorry."

"It happens."

Lacey shot Joelle a troubled glance and for a moment she chewed on her lip, struggling to find the right words to say. "I think he did love you."

"It was lust, not love," Joelle corrected roughly, and the sudden bitterness in her voice made the lump return to her throat. She felt so hurt…so confused. "I mean, how could it be love? We knew each other for only ten days. You don't fall in love in ten days."

"Those were a pretty intense ten days."

Joelle tried to shrug it off but she couldn't quite hide the hurt. "Everything with Leo was intense," she said at last, lifting her beer bottle and taking a quick drink.

Lacey said nothing and Joelle glanced at her. Lacey was still leaning forward, her blue eyes narrowed, red curly hair even curlier with the humidity.

"Besides, he had no idea what I wanted…needed." Joelle took a quick breath, steadied her voice. She wasn't going to cry, wasn't going to fall apart. She'd loved Leo's body but she wanted more than his body. She wanted his heart. His respect. His faith in her. And without those, the incredible physical attraction, that dizzying chemistry, meant nothing. "I thought I could marry out of duty, obligation, but I was wrong. I thought I could be a contract bride, but I didn't know me. I didn't realize how important it is to me to be loved for me. To have someone want me for me…not my title or my country."

Thunder boomed in the distance and Joelle sighed, the warm moist air as heavy and oppressive as her thoughts. She forced herself to shrug, to mentally move on. "So the wedding's off. The engagement's over. And I'm ready to get back to work. Get on with my life."

"And this time you're here with your grandfather's blessing?"

"Grandpapa agreed that I could use another year or two out on my own."

"Your sisters?"

"They understand, far more than I thought they would. Both Nic and Chantal struggled with the same things I did. I just didn't know. We never talked about it." Joelle took a deep breath, pushed her long hair from her eyes. "It's hot. I'd forgotten how hot it gets here in summer."

"Like a wet oven," Lacey agreed, tilting back in her own chair. She shot Joelle a curious glance. "I have to admit, Jo, I still don't get this whole arranged marriage thing. Would you have really married him if circumstances had been different…if he'd been different?"

Joelle stared out over the street, the dark clouds banking, preparing for the afternoon thunder shower. "I don't know," she said after a moment. "I thought I could do it…marry out of duty, marry because it was what I was supposed to do, but I don't know now. I'm not who I thought I was. I'm—" and she smiled, but it felt tight, painful "—a lot stronger than I thought. Tougher, too. I can't be anyone but me, and as corny as it sounds, only I know what's best for me."

Thunder boomed again and Lacey and Joelle headed back into the apartment just as the clouds overhead burst open. As she closed the doors to the balcony, Joelle suddenly wished she and Lacey hadn't talked, wished Leo's name hadn't come up because she couldn't think about him. Couldn't let herself feel. It was better to forget him—completely.

Joelle had no problem getting her job back at Club Bleu and after a couple weeks she was back in the old routine.

The routine was good for her, too, the singing and performing kept her busy, focused. When she was on stage she forgot about everything, including her own shattered heart.

The hours off stage were the hard ones. Getting through summer was brutal, but then autumn arrived, and the intense heat began to ease, and by winter Joelle felt almost human.

She still had days that hit her from behind, knocking the air out of her, the pain stunning.

Joelle picked up an extra job, waitressing in a nearby restaurant, and the extra money was good, the lack of time even better. She literally ran from one job to the next, and in the meantime she socked away every dollar she could. She was learning to take care of herself, provide for herself, and it felt good paying her own bills…paying her own way. It felt good knowing she was responsible. Capable. It helped, too, living with Lacey. Lacey had such a great perspective on life, such a refreshing sense of humor.

The door to the storage room opened where Joelle sat perched on a wooden crate, a cell phone pressed to her ear. Chet, Club Bleu's manager, held up his hand. ''Josie, you're on in five.''

She nodded to Chet, indicating she'd heard him and continued listening to the voice mail left earlier by her grandfather. She'd already replayed it twice but she needed to hear it again, missing her grandfather, missing Melio. She'd gone home only once this year and it was for her twenty-third birthday. Maybe it was time for another visit.

''Josie.'' Chet was back and he shoved his watch beneath her face. ''Wake up. You're on. *Now*.''

Joelle saved the call, snapped the phone shut and stood up. ''No problem,'' she answered calmly. On the surface, nothing ruffled her. On the surface, she was New Orleans' hottest nightclub sensation, and it was easy to appear serene. Undisturbed. No one here knew who she really was. No one knew what her heart had been through. ''I'm ready.''

"You're sure?"

The corner of her mouth curved, silent, wry, catlike. "Baby," she answered, drawling a little, pegging the Southern accent, hiding as always her European roots. "I was born ready."

She took her position on stage and the lights overhead rose, circles of purple and deep blue and as Benny hit the first bass notes, Joelle felt the sultry heat of another summer night.

Opening her eyes, she grabbed the microphone and pulled it close. Club Bleu was packed tonight, every chair filled, filled because they'd all come to see her, filled because she'd become someone in New Orleans—not because of her title or family name—but because she'd earned it by hard work.

Yet Joelle found her success was bittersweet. This is what she'd come to do, and while she'd been offered a generous recording contract, the music hadn't met all her needs. Her taste of success hadn't equaled falling in love.

Don't go there, she told herself, feeling her long dark hair swing against her back, her skin warm, growing damp, don't think about what you can't control. And yet the lump returned to fill her throat and for a moment she nearly lost her composure. She had to fight for the lyrics stuck in the back of her mouth, fight for voice and sound.

She didn't understand what was wrong with her. Nothing felt right tonight. Already she was off, uncomfortable, intense emotion swamping her.

Focus, Jo, she told herself, focus and get through the song. Nothing had changed, nothing was any different, but something inside her keep telling her everything was different.

Everything felt fierce. Intense.

Closing her eyes, Joelle clasped the microphone with both hands, fingers bending protectively, the stainless steel both cool and warm. With microphone pulled forward, tilting it on the stand, Joelle gave it all up to the night, singing about the heartache she'd never talk about in daylight.

Spotlighted by blue and purple gel lights, she admitted what she'd never admit to anyone else.

She still missed Leo. Still dreamed about him nearly every night. She'd gone out with other guys in the past year, kissed her share of men, but none of them had been Leo.

At least you have your music, she reminded herself, no one

can take that away from you. And finally she was able to shut out everything but the bass and the drums and the moodiness of the night, finally she focused and let the scorching emotion pour through her, filling the club, coloring it with powerful sound.

Two hours later, the lights lifted, purple gels fading to white and gold, and the audience erupted in thundering applause. Joelle took another bow with her band but was barely conscious of the whistles. She'd been so immersed in the last song that it was taking her a minute to return to reality.

"Well done," Johnny G, the drummer said, passing her, a towel draped around his neck as he headed off stage.

"You were on tonight, baby girl," Benny added, slipping his bass guitar into his case. "You hit all the notes."

Joelle managed a smile. She'd actually felt funny tonight. Off. Maybe it was the phone call home before she'd gotten on stage, but she felt strangely emotional. Even now tears burned just beneath the surface. "Thanks. See you guys Saturday."

She crouched down to slide her guitar into its case and used the moment to mop her face, wiping away the hint of tears before it smudged her eyeliner. It's just because it's summer again, she told herself. You're just feeling nostalgic.

With guitar strap over her shoulder, Joelle forced herself off stage.

"Josie?"

The deep voice stopped her. Joelle froze, skin prickling.

She'd gone a year without hearing that voice and yet she'd heard it in her sleep, in her dreams, night after night until it made her weep into her pillow.

Slowly she looked up into his face, and he was waiting for her, waiting, and he looked right back, his dark gaze reaching into her, holding her still.

For a moment she forgot time, forgot history, forgot pain. For a moment she stood there, washed in need for him. It had been so long…she'd missed him so much. She stared at him, drinking him in, trying to see everything at once. And his dark eyes let her, his dark eyes held her, his eyes let her know what he wanted, and he wanted her. Body and soul.

Icy heat shivered up her spine and down again. Blood surged through her, flooding her face, melting the bones of her hips and knees. It was all she could do to cling to her guitar case. "Leo."

"You were amazing."

Leo's deep voice wrapped around her heart. She'd forgotten what a distinctive voice he had, so deep, so husky. "Thank you."

Silence followed. Joelle didn't know what to do, what to say. She glanced at him and then away. What was he doing here? It stunned her, him appearing like this. It had been a year without a word, without a single phone call. Why was he here, now?

"How are you?" he asked.

"Fine." She swallowed. "And you?"

"Fine." His lips curved in a wry smile. "You're very polite."

"We're friends, right? Not enemies." But there was a hint of bitterness in her voice and he heard it.

"Friends," he repeated softly, but his green eyes were dark, hard, intense. Everything about him was hard and intense. "Can I take you to dinner?"

Her heart did a funny little beat. "I can't. I've an early morning."

"I see."

His features grew harder. Joelle's heart did another painful stagger and she changed her grip on her guitar case. "I waitress at Brennan's on Sunday mornings. You remember Brennan's?" She saw him nod and she hurried on. "Breakfast at Brennan's is famous. It's quite busy in the mornings. Frantic, really. They run me off my feet."

"I'll have to try it sometime."

Her eyes burned. "I should go."

"You're not walking home, are you?"

"It's just a couple blocks."

His jaw tightened and she saw he was biting back criticism. "I'll walk you home," he said at length. "Give me your guitar."

"Leo—" She broke off when she saw his expression. "Okay."

They walked in silence, the night still sweltering, the clouds banked, the humidity rising. It'd have to rain soon. The air felt saturated with moisture.

On reaching Joelle's apartment building, Leo escorted her up the stairs. There was an awkward moment on her doorstep after Joelle had turned the key. "Do you want to come in?" she asked stiltedly.

He'd heard that, too. "Maybe another time," he answered, turning away. "Good night."

Inside her apartment Joelle shut and locked the door.

He was gone. She should have felt relieved. Instead she felt heartsick.

She shouldn't have let him go.

She should have asked him to stay.

She should have opened a glass of wine and got them talking, really talking. She should have—

No, it was better this way.

Tears filled her eyes. Why was it better this way? What was better?

She drew a breath, tried to calm herself, but she felt lost.

Leo was here. He was *here*. And she let him go.

The pain staggered her, the pain more livid than ever. It's okay, she told herself, it's okay, this is just life, this is just love, this is how it's going to be.

But deep down inside she didn't want it to be true, because when she looked at him tonight, all she felt was want and hope and...

Need.

*Need.*

The forceful knock on the door made her heart lurch all over again. He'd come back! Relief swept through her and Joelle struggled with the lock. Emotions chaotic she swung the door open but it wasn't Leo on the doorstep, it was Lacey.

"Thank goodness you're home," Lacey said, exhaling with a rush. "I lost my key earlier and was afraid I'd be locked out."

Morning came far too early and Joelle dragged herself from bed, into the shower, out of the shower and into a jean skirt and T-shirt—she always changed into her uniform at work—and grabbed a cup of coffee in the kitchen.

"Hey." Lacey was already up, her curls wild from bed-head hair. "You okay? I haven't seen you look this blue since... well...last June."

Joelle topped her coffee with milk and dumped in a huge spoon of sugar without making eye contact. It had been a long night, a hellish night. "Didn't sleep well."

"Anything happen last night?"

"No. Why?"

"Just wondering."

Joelle downed her coffee and left the apartment, the morning temperature already in the mid-eighties. As she walked the six blocks to Brennan's she wondered why she couldn't tell Lacey about Leo's surprise appearance. Maybe it was because she still hadn't come to grips with his appearance, either. It didn't make sense that he was here, had come to see her, unless...

Unless...

But Joelle couldn't go there, wouldn't let herself go there and once she reached the restaurant was immediately sucked into the frenetic pace of breakfast with a gourmet spin. Brennan's served three-course and five-course breakfasts, as well as famous breakfast libations like Gin Fizzes, Mimosas, Bloody Marys, and the outrageous Mr. Funk of New Orleans.

By the time she'd finished her shift it was nearly two in the afternoon and she was dead on her feet. She'd thought of Leo, but not excessively, and after changing back into her skirt and T-shirt, she stepped out the back door, waved goodbye to the line cooks standing in the brick alley having a quick smoke. It wasn't until she reached the end of the alley that she noticed Leo.

He'd been waiting for her in front of Brennan's, positioned in such a place that he could see her from all the restaurant exits.

She'd half expected to see him, but hadn't expected the fierce jolt of recognition, the electric zing of nerves. He was so familiar and yet so not. So much a part of her and yet so much still hurt when she looked at him, when she thought of him. The emotion had never gentled. The loss had never eased.

"You're not working at Club Bleu tonight," he said, walking toward her, a gorgeous primal grace in just the way he moved.

She'd forgotten that about him, forgotten his grace, his sensuality, his European sophistication. But she couldn't do this, couldn't just hand herself over to him. It had been easy forgiving him, brutal forgetting him, and clearly from the way her body was responding, she hadn't succeeded in distancing herself from him at all.

"I know you're free now," he added, standing over her.

"You're not working again until morning, and Lacey said she was certain you had no plans for this afternoon."

Joelle felt hot, dizzy. Just standing this close to Leo was murder. It didn't help that the afternoon temperature had soared twenty-plus degrees since morning and the dark blanket of clouds overhead pushed the humidity past the point of comfort. Perspiration beaded her skin. Even the air was hard to breathe. "When did you see Lacey?"

"Yesterday when I arrived in town."

"She didn't tell me."

"I asked her not to."

The air seemed to grow thicker, and heavier. Quieter, too. "She's supposed to be my friend."

"She is."

Their eyes locked, another silent battle of wills. Things hadn't changed, Joelle thought, biting her tongue to keep from saying something sharp. He was still trying to dictate everything. Control her.

"Then she should have told me you were here," Joelle repeated, feeling cornered. She hated feeling cornered, especially if it was by him.

"Joelle."

"What?" she flashed, shooting a nervous glance up at the sky. It had become too quiet. It was as if the black clouds overhead had swallowed all sound. It was going to rain soon.

"Never mind. I'm not going to force this, *bella*."

She couldn't look at him, trying to sort through her tangled emotions. In the distance thin white lines ran from the sky, fragments of far away lightning, but so far nothing seemed close.

Except for Leo. He was close, far too close, and with the odd white line illuminating the sky she felt fear.

If he touched her she'd be lost. If he touched her, she'd melt straight into him.

She took a deep breath, tried to be objective. "I don't know how to do this. I've worked so hard to forget you that..." She shook her head, without words. "That it's agony seeing you. It's not something I thought would ever happen."

"You knew I loved you."

"But you left."

"We both know why."

Her throat swelled close and she felt close to tears. The afternoon had gone so dark and quiet she knew the afternoon storm was imminent.

"Want to go inside?" Leo asked, indicating the café on the corner, if one wanted to call it a café.

She knew the café. It was more like a tavern or saloon, the interior dark and cool, fans whirling on the ceiling and music blaring from a jukebox. She'd never liked the café. It served stale soda, flat beer and old popcorn. "Not particularly."

Thunder rumbled across the sky, a slow insistent roll of sound. "It's going to rain."

Joelle glanced a little helplessly out on the street. They'd walked a couple blocks from Brennan's but they were still a couple blocks from her apartment. And he was right. It would rain soon. The street was nearly deserted. Everyone knew the rain was coming, even the tourists. And when it rained in New Orleans, it flooded. They hadn't had a proper rain in days and today promised to be a torrential downpour.

If they were going to make a run for it, they had to do it now. In a minute it could be too late.

"Let's just go to my place," she said, pulling her purse higher on her shoulder.

Then she felt it. The first fat ping.

And then another. And another.

Leo grabbed her elbow, pulled her after him to the café's covered patio as the rain started coming down, hard, and harder.

In less than thirty seconds the shower became a fog, the summer rain so thick and blurry that sheets of steam rose from the street. The water slapped the pavement, bounced from the asphalt.

Like that, the streets were clear. The French Quarter became a ghost town. Cars disappeared. Pedestrians were gone. Shops had all closed their doors.

It was extraordinary. Everyone was gone, leaving just Joelle and Leo alone to watch the pounding rain.

"We might as well get something to drink," Leo said. "It's going to be awhile."

She shot him a frustrated glance. "You're glad we're stuck here."

"Try to think of me as a peace offering," he suggested dryly.

Her hands clenched. "Then why aren't I feeling peaceful?"

He laughed softly, eyes glinting. "That's something only you can answer, *bambina*. Come," he said, holding the door. "Let's find a table before we're drenched.

They ordered bowls of spicy gumbo and glasses of cold white wine at the bar counter and then found seats in a far corner. The café was just as deserted as the street and except for one old man in the corner, they had the place to themselves. "This isn't a sign of good business," Joelle whispered to Leo as they sat down.

"No, but it is dry."

The gumbo wasn't the best Joelle ever had but it filled her up, took the edge off her appetite and at least the wine was chilled. After the bartender cleared away their dishes she went to the door, stared out at the flooded streets. New Orleans had huge drains at every corner but not even the monster drains could handle the slashing rain once it started. From where she stood gutters and downspouts looked like fountains and the lone pedestrian's umbrella had turned inside out.

"Pretty bad out there," she said, sitting down again, trying not to fidget. She felt so hot, unbearably wound up.

"I guess we've got some time to kill."

# CHAPTER THIRTEEN

JOELLE felt his enjoyment as his dark green gaze rested on her face, and she could have sworn he was smiling, secretly savoring her misery.

"You planned this," she said, crossing her arms over her chest, trying her best to create distance. Detachment. She hated the way she was feeling…tingly, edgy, all bittersweet emotion. It had been so hard to forget him that she couldn't bear to sit this close now.

Leo's dark gaze gleamed. His teeth flashed white in a pure predatory smile. "I did. I arranged for the thunderstorm when I made my hotel reservations."

She glanced away, fidgeted, unable to return his intense gaze. He was studying her, closely, possessively, and everything in her seemed to unfold, come painfully to life. "We can't just sit here."

"Why not?"

Her teeth ground together and she felt such a welling of need. It wasn't fair that he still looked gorgeous. Wasn't fair that when he focused on her he made her feel like the only woman alive. Wasn't fair that his gaze made her grow hot, tense, hungry. "Because this is miserable."

"I'm comfortable."

She shot him a dark glance. "I'm not. I don't trust you."

"You never have." His teeth flashed yet again and a ripple of unease raced through her

He was bigger than she'd remembered, stronger, more physical. She'd remembered her desire, but not the effect he'd had on her, and somehow, sitting across this tiny bar table, the tavern smelling of beer and stale popcorn she felt incredibly threatened.

He represented everything she wanted. He also represented everything she feared.

He'd change her world. If she let him close enough, he'd

make her his again, and Leo's possession was like nothing she'd ever known. If he should even touch her, she feared for the safety of the walls she'd put up against him, doubted the defenses erected around her heart.

"Did my grandfather send you?" she asked bitterly, balling her hands, arms still pressed tightly against her chest as if she could somehow shut him out, keep her heart safe.

"No."

"Does he know you're here?"

One of Leo's black eyebrows lifted ever so slightly. "No. Did I need to get his permission to visit?"

Her chest squeezed tight, pulled like a rubber band and Joelle briefly closed her eyes, trying to deny the sting of pain. "So what do you want?"

"What do you think, *bella?*"

Her heart twisted yet again, her knuckles pressed tighter to her breasts, her skin soft, her insides hot, livid with emotion...hopes...hurt...dreams. "You can't have me."

"Of course I can. I was meant for you—"

"No."

"Just as you were meant for me."

"Rubbish."

He laughed softly, the husky sound filling her ears, rubbing like the pad of his thumb across her heightened senses. "I let you have time, *bella*. I never let go of you."

Her lashes lifted and she stared at him with disbelief, even as her nails bit into her palms. "It's been a year, Leo, a year. There's no relationship anymore, there's no engagement, no wedding—"

"Not yet."

"Not ever."

"You still want me as much as I want you."

She averted her head, fury making her see red, fury stealing her words, her voice, her breath. How could he do this? How could he come here and sit and make such arrogant statements? How could he even make such assumptions in the first place? "You have no idea what I want."

"No?" He drawled the word so quietly the hair at her nape rose.

Chest on fire she forced herself to lift her chin, meet his mocking gaze. "No," she drawled in reply, matching his tone, matching his taunting edge.

He wasn't going to do it to her again…overwhelm her, steamroll her, use her body against her. This time she was awake. Aware. If he truly wanted her, cared for her, then he'd win her by her heart, not by her senses.

"Let me tell you a story," he said.

She nearly laughed. "I don't think so."

"It's an interesting story."

"I doubt it."

His eyes narrowed, his gaze riveted to her face as fine creases fanned from his eyes, accenting the height of his cheekbones, the hard line of his jaw. "You're giving away your hand, *bambina.* You're revealing too much. If you hope to prove yourself indifferent, then you need less emotion. You need to show indifference."

She flushed and said nothing, seeing where he was going with this and knowing he was right, but knowing he was right didn't help. "So tell me your story," she said, trying to affect nonchalance.

His lower lip curved in the faintest smile of amusement. "You have to promise me that you won't say anything, and you won't interrupt."

Not that again. Joelle could scarcely keep her expression blank. "Fine."

Triumph flared in his eyes. "Once upon a time, not so many years ago, there was a girl named Josette Destinee d'Ville, better known as Star. Star came from a very poor family outside Baton Rouge—"

"I've heard this story."

"But she had an incredible voice and big dreams," he continued as if never interrupted. "No one worked harder than Star and eventually she became America's biggest pop singer. And then at the height of her career, Star met a handsome prince, they fell in love and she moved to Europe with him, giving up her career.''

Joelle's stomach cramped. She felt queasy. ''This isn't my favorite story.''

''It gets better.''

''I don't think so.''

''I do.'' Leo leaned forward, lifted a long tendril of her hair and slipped it behind her ear. She flinched but he kept on talking. ''Since you know this story, you're aware that Star had two little girls, princesses named Chantal and Nicolette, and Star and her prince loved their children very much. But Star didn't feel complete—''

''Because she missed her music.''

Leo smiled. ''No. She wanted one more child, one more Ducasse baby. And Star spent the next six years trying to make this very special baby. She was pregnant three more times and she lost all three babies late in the pregnancy, and after the third miscarriage the doctor told her there could be no more.''

Joelle lifted her chin, lips pressing thin. Leo saw the hurt and pain in her eyes, saw the shimmer of tears of all the years she'd felt alone.

Lightly he touched Joelle's cheek. She didn't flinch this time, didn't pull back.

''But Star couldn't accept that there'd be no third child. She wanted this child, couldn't explain it to Julien, couldn't explain it to anyone. But Star couldn't have another baby so her prince tried to distract her, tried to push her back into music—he built her a studio, drove her to start writing music again—but Star didn't want music. She wanted a baby. There was one more baby for her, one more and she knew it.''

Tears filled Joelle's eyes and her lower lip quivered but she ruthlessly she bit into the lip.

''And against the doctors orders, Star became pregnant again. It was a difficult pregnancy, as difficult as the others but she refused to lose the baby, and she fought for that baby every step of the way. Nine months later Star delivered the most beautiful baby girl of all, and Prince Julien and Star named this miracle baby Joelle. And Star, with all her many accomplishments, and all her staggering successes, finally felt complete.''

Joelle couldn't look at him anymore, couldn't bear any of it. The tears streamed down her cheeks and struggled to wipe them away but there were more tears than hands and she choked on a sob, feeling naked, stricken. She couldn't do this, fall apart like this in front of Leo.

"No wonder you're so driven to be you," he said gently. "You have your mother's heart—and all her dreams and wishes—inside of you."

She covered her mouth with her hand, knowing she couldn't keep the staggering emotion in, knowing she was about to break, burst, knowing she'd spent too long trying to be strong and independent, trying to be okay on her own. But she'd been lonely. And it'd been hard. And she missed home and she missed her parents and she missed family.

She missed loving and being loved.

She missed romance, missed fire, missed ice.

Missed Leo more than she could ever say.

Suddenly Leo was pulling her into his arms, holding her close against him. "You deserve better," he said, holding her close to his chest. "You deserved better from me."

She couldn't answer, couldn't find words to express any of the inarticulate emotion flooding her. It had been such a hard year, a long, lonely year. And while of course part of her hoped she'd see him again, she hadn't honestly thought they'd ever have another chance. She'd started to think their relationship had been just chemistry, a sexy pull that had nothing to do with their hearts, their emotional needs, and yet Leo was here, holding her, his arms wrapped around her, his heartbeat steady beneath her ear.

She buried her wet face against his neck not wanting to think, just feel, and he felt warm, smelled delicious, a heady mix of spicy cologne and endless gorgeous skin. No one had ever held her the way he did. No one had ever made her feel half so alive.

Her hand balled helplessly against his chest. "I missed you."

"It was hell to stay away."

Dragging in a breath, Joelle knew she'd never get tired of his scent, of his strength, of the way he looked at her and made her burn, made her feel so much. "Then why did you?"

She felt his shoulders shift, muscles tightening through his chest, arms like hard bands and he brought her even closer against him. "I had things to work through."

"Like what?" Her voice broke, the hurt and need showing through.

"Like coming to grips with my past. Accepting the fact that I've been very angry with my mother, that I needed to deal with that anger or it'd ruin the future." His hand slid up her nape, wrapped her hair around his hand, held the impromptu ponytail snugly. "That it was already destroying the relationship I wanted with you."

She could hardly breathe, hardly force the air into her lungs, concentrating so hard on the words echoing around inside her head.

"I'm ashamed I put that surveillance band on you, *bella*. I'm ashamed that I hurt you, controlled you. I was just so desperate—so determined—not to lose you. Loving you so much filled me with fear."

Loving you so much...

Loving you...

She closed her eyes against the hot rush of tears. "You love me?"

Fingertips stroked her nape, drawing slow gentle circles so that she tingled from head to toe. "More than I thought I could love anyone." He hesitated. "More than I wanted to love anyone."

Her hands gripped his shirt, squeezing the fabric in fists. He was saying the words she needed, the words she'd craved and yet...and yet...she was afraid, afraid to hope, afraid to believe.

"I've learned a lot this year," he added, "I've worked hard to come to peace with my mother, forgiving her for that which she did, for that which she couldn't give, and I'm ready for a future with you, ready for the life I want to live with you."

"This is about Melio, isn't it?"

He laughed, a low stricken laugh that sounded torn from him. "*Bella,* I'm a disgustingly wealthy man with more chateaus and schlosses and villas than I know what to do with. I don't need Melio or Mejia. I don't need another island—I've one of my own off the coast of Sicily. But I do need you. I love you. I don't want to go to bed anymore without kissing you good night. I don't want to wake up without having you there next to me. I don't want a life alone.''

"I'm sure women are crazy about you," she sniffed, trying to stop the tears welling in her eyes.

"But I want the woman who drove me crazy," he said, lifting up her chin to wipe the tears from her face. "I want the woman who made me grow up, face myself, face my fears. You changed me, made me stronger, kinder, made me real. And there's too much here…too much we feel to let it go without a fight. I'm fighting for us now, Joelle. And I'll keep fighting. Tell me you'll fight, too.''

She searched his eyes, searched his heart and she saw a man unguarded, a man with a strong lovely face, a strong angled jaw, but a man without the hardness, the bitterness, the edges. The anger was gone.

"I'd like to fight for us," she said after a moment, "I want to believe in us…''

"But?"

"You're older than me."

He was trying hard to look serious. "By at least twelve years.''

"And as you said, you're disgustingly wealthy."

"This is true. While most women enjoy a certain lifestyle— clothes, travel, cars and jewelry—I get the sense you don't.''

She nodded. "I find the whole idea of providing a woman with a lifestyle offensive. I don't want to be given a lifestyle. I want a relationship.''

There was a moment of silence.

She licked her lips, mouth drying, heart pounding harder. He was looking at her like a wolf eyeing a little lamb. He'd have her. She knew he'd have her.

"Trust me, *bella*," he said, breaking the tense silence, "you'd get a relationship.''

She heard the possession in his voice and it sent shudders through her.

"Perhaps," he added, "the real issue is that you're not attracted to me."

"Not attracted?"

"Perhaps the physical spark is gone."

The husky, teasing note in his voice sent blood surging, and shivers tingling all the way through her. Not attracted? No physical spark? It would be easy if that were the problem.

"Tell me you're not attracted and I'll leave you alone," he persisted, and yet his dark green eyes heated, a dangerous light flaming there.

Hot. Primal. Sexual.

Her heart slammed into her rib cage. "I'm not attracted."

He smiled. His eyes creased at the corner. "Okay." And then he set out to prove how wrong she was.

He kissed her as the rain poured down, kissed her until she couldn't think, couldn't breathe, couldn't see, kissed her until she was sure he'd stolen all the pain from her, taking it away with his lips and breath, and when he lifted his head, he was smiling faintly, mockingly. "I understand you, *bella,* far better than you think."

Somehow her hands had slid down his chest and rested on his hip bones, holding him steady, holding him, holding him as if she'd never let him go. She put her hands up against his chest to push him away. "What do you know?" she breathed.

"That all you've ever wanted is to be like everyone else. That for once you want to feel like everyone else."

Joelle's heart did a funny twist. The words were familiar, they sounded exactly like her thoughts.

"You want to wear jeans and boots and tennis shoes. Leather coats with lots of fringe."

Those *were* her words, the words she'd written earlier this year and turned into a song. *I want to go to a bar and sit with a beer and get drunk in public if I want...* "You've been listening to my lyrics," she said, frowning at him and then ruining the effect by bursting into laughter. "I can't believe anyone would listen that closely."

"I thought it was about time I paid attention to what you were telling me, thought if we were going to have a chance at succeeding, I needed to get to know you, the real you, the you that's meant to be."

His words made her eyes sting hot all over again and glancing out, past his shoulder she saw the rain was starting to let up, the downpour turning to steamy mist. "You want to know *me*."

"Yes, you, the real you, the you I fell in love with a year ago."

"You didn't like the real me."

He laughed, kissed her. "I loved the real you, even if you were dressed like a sex kitten."

A ray of sun broke through the clouds, a sharp bright streak of yellow white light. "And what's wrong with a sex kitten?"

He muttered something in Italian and then tangling his hand in her hair again, drew her face close, very close to his so that his warm breath caressed her cheeks, her skin, her lips. "Nothing, *bambina*. As long as she's mine."

Suddenly a crease darkened his brow, his eyes narrowing, his jaw jutting. "You are mine, aren't you?"

The ray of sun outside pierced the tavern's gloom, spreading light into every dark corner, the light so bright it nearly blinded Joelle. Wrapping her arms around Leo's neck she put her lips to his ears. "Of course. I've been yours from the moment you first looked at you—yours from the word go."

"The word go?"

Her arms wrapped tighter. She held him closer, held him with all her strength, all her passion, feeling so much. "Make that, hello."

She lifted her head, searched his eyes, saw the brilliant light outside there in his sexy green eyes. "I love you, Leo."

"I know."

# EPILOGUE

"WE'RE late," Joelle said for the tenth time in as many minutes. "I can't be late. I don't want to be late."

Nic and Chantal shot her amused but exasperated glances. "If you hadn't started crying, you wouldn't have had to redo your makeup," Chantal said.

"If someone had told me about the veil earlier, I wouldn't have cried."

"You would have still cried," Nic answered, reaching over to straighten the veil. "You look beautiful, Jo. That tiara was made for you."

Joelle reached up to touch the delicate diamond tiara, the tiara in the shape of five brilliant stars supported on a gallery of diamond-studded foliage. Her father, Prince Julien, had commissioned the tiara for his wedding to Star and the tiara had been put away ever since.

Joelle blinked madly, her fingers tracing one sharp star. To think the tiara had been saved for her. All these years. Waiting for her own wedding day and suddenly she didn't think she could keep the tears back another moment longer and using the tip of a gloved finger she dashed away another hot tear. "I'm falling apart!" she choked in protest.

"It's okay, Aunt Joelle." Lilly scooted across the seat, out from beneath her mother's arm to squeeze closer to Joelle. "Brides are supposed to cry."

Joelle laughed, and hugged Lilly back even as she swiped the tears from beneath her lashes. "How do you know so much about life, Lilly?"

Lilly heaved a sigh. "I'm eight now, Aunt Jo. You lost track of time when you and Prince Leo were having all those attitude issues."

Chantal shushed Lilly but Nic laughed and Joelle shot her sisters a wry glance. "Thanks, Lilly. I remember now."

Any other time the drive from the palace to the cathedral would have taken minutes, but with the crowds lining the streets, the driver of their classic cream Rolls-Royce limousine was forced to creep through the old streets of downtown, allowing the crowds on the pavement a chance to see the three Princess Ducasses.

They'd made it, Joelle realized, feeling a lump fill her throat. Somehow, someway they'd survived the leap from girlhood to adulthood and they were happy. Healthy. Safe.

The car drew to a stop in front of the cathedral, the back door opened, the long crimson carpet unfurled, and Joelle leaned forward to impulsively press a kiss to each of her sister's cheeks. "Thank you," she whispered, grateful, touched, incredibly moved to have them with her today. *Her* wedding day. She'd always been the youngest princess, the last of the Ducasse girls, but somehow it felt different…she felt different…she'd changed in the past couple of years. She was ready to belong to Melio again, ready for her future here.

As she stepped from the Rolls-Royce she heard someone cry, "We love you, Princess Jo!"

And the crowds thronging the cathedral picked up the shout, chanting her name as Grandpapa slowly came down the steps, leaning on his cane to take her arm.

"They love you," her grandfather said.

She nodded, her chest burning with emotion. Everyone had been so good to her, so patient, and she was more grateful than anyone would know. "I love them, too," she said, and shifting her bridal bouquet of white lilies, tulips and freesias to her other arm, she lifted a shy hand, acknowledging the cheers.

"They're glad you're home," King Remi added.

She waved to the crows on the other side of the street, smiling as the cheers swelled in volume. "So am I, Grandpapa."

They climbed the front steps of the cathedral, entered the great stone church through dark arched doors, and yet once inside the cathedral the dark stained wood gave way to lavender and white arches supported by gray and white marble columns, the floor a dark rose marble, and the altar a half circle with a dozen stained-glass windows, each window surrounded by the finest white plaster friezes, the detail breathtaking.

Joelle knew the cathedral well. Here her parents and grandparents had been buried, her sisters married, and little Lilly baptized. She knew each of the arches, all the knaves, the choir stalls, the confessionals, but nothing touched her more than the man waiting for her before the altar.

Leo.

He stood waiting for her, flanked by two distinguished groomsmen—Malik Nuri, the Sultan of Baraka, and Demetrius Mantheakis, Greek tycoon who answered to no one, and he was everything she'd ever wanted, everything she'd ever dreamed about.

Prince Leo Fortino Marciano Borgarde. Her heart.

With organ playing and hundreds of candles shimmering, Joelle watched Nic and Chantal and then Lilly precede her down the aisle.

And then it was her turn. At long last. Three years after her engagement to her prince and two years after losing her virginity to him.

She felt wobbly as she walked with her grandfather. Grandpapa needed to walk slowly, and yet he was beaming, infinitely proud. Her own heart pounded with each slow, deliberate step. Life hadn't ever been easy and yet each lesson learned had brought her to this.

She was shaking by the time she and her grandfather finally reached the front of the cathedral, and looking up at her dear grandpapa, a man who'd had to become grandfather and father as well as king, she realized she'd survived the long journey—not just walking the endless white carpeted aisle—but the three years it took to grow up properly, the last year with Leo where they both learned how to love properly, like not to hold grudges, to let an argument die, to gracefully accept an apology.

Her gloved hand squeezed Grandpapa's arm. "Thank you," she whispered, just before he placed her hand in Leo's. "I owe you everything."

"You owe me nothing. Just be happy."

"I am."

Grandpapa kissed her cheek and then he was gone, leaving her in Leo's care and the significance took her breath away, squeezing the air inside her.

The organ died. The bishop began addressing the assembly. "I'm late," she whispered, stealing a glance up at Leo's profile.

"Just a half hour," he whispered back.

She gripped his arm more tightly. "Sorry."

His hand covered hers. He was warm and his warmth relaxed her. "I'm getting good at waiting."

She nearly laughed. She shouldn't laugh. It was her wedding day. She was marrying a prince. Life was getting quite serious now. "You've become a very patient man."

The corner of his mouth lifted. "Why not? We all need some extra time now and then."

The next couple of hours whirled by, music, color, words and sound. And Joelle enjoyed all of it, the ceremony, the reception, the dinner, the dancing but at last it was time for her and Leo to escape. And they escaped to the room at the Palace Hotel that Leo had booked. Tomorrow they'd leave on their two-week Greek cruise, but the rest of the night was theirs and with security at the hotel tight, they were assured a night without any interruptions.

Joelle sat down before the mirror at the dressing table and worked at unpinning the headpiece but it wasn't coming off. "Leo, can you give me a hand? I don't want to tear the veil."

He appeared from the bathroom. She heard water running. He was filling the tub. And in the mirror their eyes met. He was smiling, that dark sexual smile that sent shivers up and down her spine even now.

Silently he crossed the bedroom carpet, his gaze in the mirror never leaving hers. "You're beautiful."

Her heart raced, pulses leaping even as she went liquid on the inside, all hot fire and desire.

He'd moved behind her, one hand brushing her bare shoulders and she sighed, lips parting.

The corner of his mouth lifted and yet he set to work unfastening the headpiece one pin at a time. "It's a beautiful tiara," he said, adroitly freeing the veil and tiara and handing it to her.

Joelle tilted the delicate tiara, the five brilliant stars glittering. "Grandpapa had been saving it for me."

"Your family loves you."

She nodded, bit her lip, overwhelmed by emotion. She felt so lucky, so blessed. Everything good and lovely had come true, all the heartache and heartbreak, none of it seemed real anymore. None of it mattered.

And suddenly she felt a prickle of heat, a rush of energy and glancing up, she discovered Leo looking at her.

Just as he loved her, she thought, feeling his love wash over her, through her, his love so tangible, so visible there in his eyes.

Maybe this is what made life with Leo so intense, so exciting. All he had to do was look at her and she felt him, wanted him, and the desire wasn't diminishing but growing stronger with time.

"You've gone quiet on me," she whispered, her neck feeling bare, her breasts aching, even her lips feeling strangely full, nerves dancing.

His gaze drifted slowly across her face, taking in every bare place of her skin that felt so bereft of his touch, so hungry for his lips.

Her skin warmed, growing pink and flushed even as her tummy knotted again and again, the surge of desire and adrenaline becoming painful.

"I'm just watching you," he said.

True, and the energy between them felt electric. "You really did fight for me."

"I had no choice."

"Why?"

The corner of his mouth tugged. His expression gentled, his green gaze heating. "You already know the answer."

She went to his side, still dressed in her white wedding gown, the silk cool, light against her legs. "I want to hear it again."

He sat down on the edge of the bed, and pulled her down next to him. "I love you."

"Again."

"I love you."

"Again."

"I love you."

And then leaning close, she kissed him, slowly, hungrily, savoring the desire rising through them. "Promise me you'll never stop telling me you love me."

"I promise."

"And promise me you'll still love me even when we're old and gray."

"I promise."

"And promise you'll always remember today."

He laughed, the sound husky. "I promise."

She drew a deep breath, still trying to absorb it all. "You know, we've got the most incredible story to tell our children."

"They won't believe it."

"They'll have to. It's the story of you and me."

"Quite a story," he teased.

"Larger than life."

"Full of stubbornness and one very hothead—"

She kissed him, cutting off his words. "You're describing yourself, of course."

He laughed again, very low and sexy. "Perhaps we need to agree on the story…get the facts right."

"I agree. In fact, maybe while we're on our honeymoon we can start going over the details…agree to agree…agree to disagree as well."

"*Bella,* I think we have time."

"Not that much time." And leaning closer, she pressed her lips to his and whispered, "I'm pregnant. We're expecting a Christmas baby."

# HARLEQUIN®
## *Presents*

**Seduction and Passion Guaranteed!**

INTERNATIONAL DOCTORS

**They're guaranteed
to raise your pulse!**

Meet the most eligible medical men in the world in a
new series of stories by popular authors that
will make your heart race!

Whether they're saving lives or dealing with desire,
our doctors have bedside manners that send
temperatures soaring....

**Coming December 2004:**

# The Italian's Passionate Proposal
## by Sarah Morgan

### #2437

Also, don't miss more medical stories
guaranteed to set pulses racing.

Promotional Presents features the
**Mediterranean Doctors** Collection in May 2005.

*Available wherever Harlequin books are sold.*

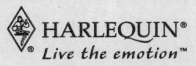

# HARLEQUIN®
*Live the emotion*™

**www.eHarlequin.com**                    HPINTDOC